W9-DDP-314

DEATH SWOOPS ON BAT WINGS

"Not a sound if you value your life!" he warned. "In a moment or two, he will come into this room, either through the door or by that window. Don't you understand? There's a *killer* loose!"

They all stood there, waiting for they knew not what. Only Miss Cornelia's agile brain seemed able to respond.

"I begin to understand," she said. "The man who killed Dick Fleming and stabbed that poor wretch in the closet—the man who started that fire outside— is—"

"Sssh! Stand back out of that light!"

A black bulk, masked and sinister, stood clearly outlined against the diminishing glow of the fire.

The Bat!

MASTERWORKS OF MYSTERY
BY MARY ROBERTS RINEHART!

THE YELLOW ROOM   (2262, $3.50)

The somewhat charred corpse unceremoniously stored in the linen closet of Carol Spencer's Maine summer home set the plucky amateur sleuth on the trail of a killer. But each step closer to a solution led Carol closer to her own imminent demise!

THE CASE OF JENNIE BRICE   (2193, $2.95)

The bloodstained rope, the broken knife—plus the disappearance of lovely Jennie Brice—were enough to convince Mrs. Pittman that murder had been committed in her boarding house. And if the police couldn't see what was in front of their noses, then the inquisitive landlady would just have to take matters into her own hands!

THE GREAT MISTAKE   (2122, $3.50)

Patricia Abbott never planned to fall in love with wealthy Tony Wainwright, especially after she found out about the wife he'd never bothered to mention. But suddenly she was trapped in an extra-marital affair that was shadowed by unspoken fear and shrouded in cold, calculating murder!

THE RED LAMP   (2017, $3.50)

The ghost of Uncle Horace was getting frisky—turning on lamps, putting in shadowy appearances in photographs. But the mysterious nightly slaughter of local sheep seemed to indicate that either Uncle Horace had developed a bizarre taste for lamb chops . . . or someone was manipulating appearances with a deadly sinister purpose!

A LIGHT IN THE WINDOW   (1952, $3.50)

Ricky Wayne felt uncomfortable about moving in with her new husband's well-heeled family while he was overseas fighting the Germans. But she never imagined the depths of her in-laws' hatred—or the murderous lengths to which they would go to break up her marriage!

Available wherever paperbacks are sold, or order direct from the Publisher. Send cover price plus 50¢ per copy for mailing and handling to Zebra Books, Dept. 2627, 475 Park Avenue South, New York, N.Y. 10016. Residents of New York, New Jersey and Pennsylvania must include sales tax. DO NOT SEND CASH.

MARY ROBERTS RINEHART

THE BAT

ZEBRA BOOKS
KENSINGTON PUBLISHING CORP.

ZEBRA BOOKS

are published by

Kensington Publishing Corp.
475 Park Avenue South
New York, NY 10016

Copyright © 1926 by Farrar & Rinehart, Inc. Copyright
© 1954 by Mary Roberts Rinehart. This edition is re-
printed by arrangement with Henry Holt and Company
Inc.

All rights reserved. No part of this book may be repro-
duced in any form or by any means without the prior
written consent of the Publisher, excepting brief quotes
used in reviews.

Second Zebra Books printing: May, 1990

Printed in the United States of America

CONTENTS

Chapter One: The Shadow of the Bat

"You've *got* to get him, boys—get him or bust!" said a tired police chief, pounding a heavy fist on a table. The detectives he bellowed the words at looked at the floor. They had done their best and failed. Failure meant "resignation" for the police chief, return to the hated work of pounding the pavements for them—they knew it, and, knowing it, could summon no gesture of bravado to answer their chief's. Gunmen, thugs, hi-jackers, loft-robbers, murderers, they could get them all in time—but they could not get the man he wanted.

"Get him—to hell with expense—I'll give you carte blanche—but get him!" said a haggard millionaire in the sedate inner offices of the best private detective firm in the country. The man on the other side of the desk, man hunter extraordinary, old servant of Government and State, sleuthhound without a peer, threw up his hands in a gesture of odd hopelessness. "It isn't the money, Mr. De Courcy—I'd give every cent I've made to get the man you want—but I can't

7

promise you results—for the first time in my life."
The conversation was ended.

"Get him? Huh! I'll get him, watch my smoke!" It
was young ambition speaking in a certain set of
rooms in Washington. Three days later young ambition lay in a New York gutter with a bullet in his
heart and a look of such horror and surprise on his
dead face that even the ambulance-doctor who found
him felt shaken. "We've lost the most promising man
I've had in ten years," said his chief when the news
came in. He swore helplessly, "Damn the luck!"

"Get him—get him—get him—*get* him!" From a
thousand sources now the clamor arose—press, police, and public alike crying out for the capture of the
master criminal of a century—lost voices hounding a
specter down the alleyways of the wind. And still the
meshes broke and the quarry slipped away before the
hounds were well on the scent—leaving behind a trail
of shattered safes and rifled jewel cases—while ever
the clamor rose higher to "Get him—get him—get—"

Get whom, in God's name—get what? Beast, man,
or devil? A specter—a flying shadow—the shadow of
a Bat.

From thieves' hangout to thieves' hangout the word
passed along stirring the underworld like the passage
of an electric spark. "There's a bigger guy than Pete
Flynn shooting the works, a guy that could have Jim
Gunderson for breakfast and not notice he'd et." The
underworld heard and waited to be shown; after a
little while the underworld began to whisper to itself
in tones of awed respect. There were bright stars and

8

flashing comets in the sky of the world of crime—but this new planet rose with the portent of an evil moon.

The Bat—they called him the Bat. Like a bat he chose the night hours for his work of rapine; like a bat he struck and vanished, pouncingly, noiselessly; like a bat he never showed himself to the face of the day. He'd never been in stir, the bulls had never mugged him, he didn't run with a mob, he played a lone hand, and fenced his stuff so that even the Fence couldn't swear he knew his face. Most lone wolves had a moll at any rate—women were their ruin—but if the Bat had a moll, not even the grapevine telegraph could locate her.

Rat-faced gunmen in the dingy back rooms of saloons muttered over his exploits with bated breath. In tawdrily gorgeous apartments, where gathered the larger figures, the proconsuls of the world of crime, cold, conscienceless brains dissected the work of a colder and swifter brain than theirs, with suave and bitter envy. Evil's Four Hundred chattered, discussed, debated—sent out a thousand invisible tentacles to clutch at a shadow—to turn this shadow and its distorted genius to their own ends. The tentacles recoiled, baffled—the Bat worked alone—not even Evil's Four Hundred could bend him into a willing instrument to execute another's plan.

The men higher up waited. They had dealt with lone wolves before and broken them. Some day the Bat would slip and falter; then they would have him. But the weeks passed into months and still the Bat flew free, solitary, untamed, and deadly. At last even his own kind turned upon him; the underworld is like the upper in its fear and distrust of genius that flies alone. But when they turned against him, they turned against a spook—a shadow. A cold and bodiless laughter from a pit of darkness answered and mocked at their bungling gestures of hate—and went on, flouting Law and Lawless alike.

Where official trailer and private sleuth had failed, the newspapers might succeed—or so thought the disillusioned young men of the Fourth Estate—the tireless foxes, nose-down on the trail of news—the trackers, who never gave up until that news was run to earth. Star reporter, leg-man, cub, veteran gray in the trade—one and all they tried to pin the Bat like a caught butterfly to the front page of their respective journals—soon or late each gave up, beaten. He was news—bigger news each week—a thousand ticking typewriters clicked his adventures—the brief, staccato recital of his career in the morgues of the great dailies grew longer and more incredible each day. But the big news—the scoop of the century—the yearned-for headline, *Bat Nabbed Red-Handed, Bat Slain in Gun Duel with Police*—still eluded the ravenous maw of the Linotypes. And meanwhile, the red-scored list of his felonies lengthened and the rewards offered from various sources for any clue which might lead to his apprehension mounted and mounted till they totaled a small fortune.

Columnists took him up, played with the name and the terror, used the name and the terror as a starting point from which to exhibit their own particular opinions on everything and anything. Ministers mentioned him in sermons; cranks wrote fanatic letters denouncing him as one of the seven-headed beasts of the Apocalypse and a forerunner of the end of the world; a popular revue put on a special Bat number wherein eighteen beautiful chorus girls appeared masked and black-winged in costumes of Brazilian bat fur; there were Bat club sandwiches, Bat cigarettes, and a new shade of hosiery called simply and succintly *Bat*. He became a fad — a catchword — a national figure. And yet — he was walking Death — cold — remorseless. But Death itself had become a toy of publicity.

A city editor, at lunch with a colleague, pulled at his cigarette and talked. "See that Sunday story we had on the Bat?" he asked. "Pretty tidy — huh — and yet we didn't have to play it up. It's an amazing list — the Marshall jewels — the Allison murder — the mail truck thing — two hundred thousand he got out of that, all negotiable, and two men dead. I wonder how many people he's really killed. We made it six murders and nearly a million in loot — didn't even have room for the small stuff — but there must be more — "

His companion whistled.

"And when is the Universe's Finest Newspaper going to burst forth with *Bat Captured by* BLADE *Reporter?*" he queried sardonically.

"Oh, for — lay off it, will you?" said the city editor peevishly. "The Old Man's been hopping around about it for two months till everybody's plumb

11

cuckoo. Even offered a bonus—a big one—and that shows how crazy he is—he doesn't love a nickel any better than his right eye—for any sort of exclusive story. Bonus—huh!" and he crushed out his cigarette. "It won't be a *Blade* reporter that gets that bonus—or any reporter. It'll be Sherlock Holmes from the spirit world!"

"Well, can't you dig up a Sherlock?"

The editor spread out his hands. "Now, look here," he said. "We've got the best staff of any paper in the country, if I do say it. We've got boys that could get a personal signed story from Delilah on how she barbered Samson—and find out who struck Billy Patterson and who was the Man in the Iron Mask. But the Bat's something else again. Oh, of course, we've panned the police for not getting him; that's always the game. But, personally, I won't pan them; they've done their damnedest. They're up against something new. Scotland Yard wouldn't do any better—or any other bunch of cops that I know about."

"But look here, Bill, you don't mean to tell me he'll keep on getting away with it indefinitely?"

The editor frowned. "Confidentially—I don't know," he said with a chuckle. "The situation's this: for the first time the super-crook—the super-crook of fiction—the kind that never makes a mistake—has come to life—real life. And it'll take a cleverer man than any Central Office dick I've ever met to catch him!"

"Then you don't think he's just an ordinary crook with a lot of luck?"

12

"I do not." The editor was emphatic. "He's much brainier. Got a ghastly sense of humor, too. Look at the way he leaves his calling card after every job—a black paper bat inside the Marshall safe—a bat drawn on the wall with a burnt match where he'd jimmied the Cedarburg Bank—a real bat, dead, tacked to the mantelpiece over poor old Allison's body. Oh, he's in a class by himself—and I very much doubt if he was a crook at all for most of his life."

"You mean?"

"I mean this. The police have been combing the underworld for him; I don't think he comes from there. I think they've got to look higher, up in our world, for a brilliant man with a kink in the brain. He may be a doctor, a lawyer, a merchant, honored in his community by day—good line that, I'll use it some time—and at night, a bloodthirsty assassin. Deacon Brodie—ever hear of him—the Scotch deacon that burgled his parishioners' houses on the quiet? Well—that's our man."

"But my Lord, Bill—"

"I know. I've been going around the last month, looking at everybody I knew and thinking—*are you the Bat?* Try it for a while. You'll want to sleep with a light in your room after a few days of it. Look around the University Club—that white-haired man over there—dignified—respectable—is he the Bat? Your own lawyer—your own doctor—your own best friend. Can happen you know."

"Bill! You're giving me the shivers!"

"Am I?" The editor laughed grimly. "Think it over. No, it isn't so pleasant. But that's my theory — and I swear I think I'm right." He rose.

His companion laughed uncertainly.

"How about you, Bill — are you the Bat?"

The editor smiled. "See," he said, "it's got you already. No, I can prove an alibi. The Bat's been laying off the city recently — taking a fling at some of the swell suburbs. Besides I haven't the brains — I'm free to admit it." He struggled into his coat. "Well, let's talk about something else. I'm sick of the Bat and his murders."

His companion rose as well, but it was evident that the editor's theory had taken firm hold on his mind. As they went out the door together he recurred to the subject.

"Honestly, though, Bill — were you serious, really serious — when you said you didn't know of a single detective with brains enough to trap this devil?"

The editor paused in the doorway. "Serious enough," he said. "And yet there's one man — I don't know him myself but from what I have heard of him, he might be able — but what's the use of speculating?"

"I'd like to know all the same," insisted the other, and laughed nervously. "We're moving out to the country next week ourselves — right in the Bat's new territory."

"We-el," said the editor, "you won't let it go any further? Of course it's just an idea of mine, but if the Bat ever came prowling around our place, the detective I'd try to get in touch with would be—" He put his lips close to his companions's ear and whispered a name.

The man whose name he whispered, oddly enough, was at that moment standing before his official superior in a quiet room not very far away. Tall, reticently good-looking and well, if inconspicuously, clothed and groomed, he by no means seemed the typical detective that the editor had spoken of so scornfully. He looked something like a college athlete who had kept up his training, something like a pillar of one of the more sedate financial houses. He could assume and discard a dozen manners in as many minutes, but, to the casual observer, the one thing certain about him would probably seem his utter lack of connection with the seamier side of existence. The key to his real secret of life, however, lay in his eyes. When in repose, as now, they were veiled and without unusual quality—but they were the eyes of a man who can wait and a man who can strike.

He stood perfectly easy before his chief for several moments before the latter looked up from his papers.

"Well, Anderson," he said at last, looking up, "I got your report on the Wilhenry burglary this morning. I'll tell you this about it—if you do a neater and quicker job in the next ten years, you can take this desk away from me. I'll give it to you. As it is, your name's gone up for promotion today; you deserved it long ago."

"Thank you, sir," replied the tall man quietly, "but I had luck with that case."

15

"Of course you had luck," said the chief. "Sit down, won't you, and have a cigar—if you can stand my brand. Of course you had luck, Anderson, but that isn't the point. It takes a man with brains to use a piece of luck as you used it. I've waited a long time here for a man with your sort of brains and, by Judas, for a while I thought they were all as dead as Pinkerton. But now I know there's one of them alive at any rate—and it's a hell of a relief."

"Thank you, sir," said the tall man, smiling and sitting down. He took a cigar and lit it. "That makes it easier, sir—your telling me that. Because—I've come to ask a favor."

"All right," responded the chief promptly. "Whatever it is, it's granted."

Anderson smiled again. "You'd better hear what it is first, sir. I don't want to put anything over on you. I want to be assigned to a certain case—that's all."

The chief's look grew searching. "H'm," he said. "Well, as I say, anything within reason. What case do you want to be assigned to?"

The muscles of Anderson's left hand tensed on the arm of his chair. He looked squarely at the chief. "I want a chance at the Bat!" he replied slowly.

The chief's face became expressionless. "I said—anything within reason," he responded softly, regarding Anderson keenly.

"I want a chance at the Bat!" repeated Anderson stubbornly. "If I've done good work so far—I want a chance at the Bat!"

The chief drummed on the desk. Annoyance and

surprise were in his voice when he spoke.

"But look here, Anderson," he burst out finally. "Anything else and I'll—but what's the use? I said a minute ago, you had brains—but now, by Judas, I doubt it! If anyone else wanted a chance at the Bat, I'd give it to them and gladly—I'm hard-boiled. But you're too valuable a man to be thrown away!"

"I'm no more valuable than Wentworth would have been."

"Maybe not—and look what happened to him! A bullet hole in his heart—and thirty years of work that he might have done thrown away! No, Anderson, I've found two first-class men since I've been at this desk—Wentworth and you. He asked for his chance; I gave it to him—turned him over to the Government—and lost him. Good detectives aren't so plentiful that I can afford to lose you both."

"Wentworth was a friend of mine," said Anderson softly. His knuckles were white dints in the hand that gripped the chair. "Ever since the Bat got him I've wanted my chance. Now my other work's cleaned up—and I still want it."

"But I tell you—" began the chief in tones of high exasperation. Then he stopped and looked at his protégé. There was a silence for a time.

"Oh, well—" said the chief finally in a hopeless voice. "Go ahead—commit suicide—I'll send you a 'Gates Ajar' and a card, 'Here lies a damn fool who would have been a great detective if he hadn't been so pigheaded.' *Go* ahead!"

Anderson rose. "Thank you, sir," he said in a deep

voice. His eyes had light in them now. "I can't thank you enough, sir."

"Don't try," grumbled the chief. "If I weren't as much of a damned fool as you are I wouldn't let you do it. And if I weren't so damned old, I'd go after the slippery devil myself and let you sit here and watch *me* get brought in with an infernal paper bat pinned where my shield ought to be. The Bat's supernatural, Anderson. You haven't a chance in the world but it does me good all the same to shake hands with a man with brains *and* nerve," and he solemnly wrung Anderson's hand in an iron grip.

Anderson smiled. "The cagiest bat flies once too often," he said. "I'm not promising anything, chief, but — "

"Maybe," said the chief. "Now wait a minute, keep your shirt on, you're not going bat hunting this minute, you know — "

"Sir? I thought I — "

"Well, you're not," said the chief decidedly. "I've still some little respect for my own intelligence and it tells me to get all the work out of you I can, before you start wild-goose chasing after this — this bat out of hell. The first time he's heard of again — and it shouldn't be long from the fast way he works — you're assigned to the case. That's understood. Till then, you do what *I* tell you — and it'll be *work,* believe me!"

"All right, sir," Anderson laughed and turned to the door. "And — thank you again."

He went out. The door closed. The chief remained

18

for some minutes looking at the door and shaking his head. "The best man I've had in years—except Wentworth," he murmured to himself. "And throwing himself away—to be killed by a cold-blooded devil that nothing human can catch—you're getting old, John Grogan—but, by Judas, you can't blame him, can you? If you were a man in the prime like him, by Judas, you'd be doing it yourself. And yet it'll go hard—losing him—"

He turned back to his desk and his papers. But for some minutes he could not pay attention to the papers. There was a shadow on them—a shadow that blurred the typed letters—the shadow of bat's wings.

Chapter Two:
The Indomitable Miss Van Gorder

Miss Cornelia Van Gorder, indomitable spinster, last bearer of a name which has been great in New York when New York was a red-roofed Nieuw Amsterdam and Peter Stuyvesant a parvenu, sat propped up in bed in the green room of her newly rented country house reading the morning newspaper. Thus seen, with an old soft Paisley shawl tucked in about her thin shoulders and without the stately gray transformation that adorned her on less intimate occasions, she looked much less formidable and more innocently placid than those could ever have imagined who had only felt the bite of her tart wit at such functions as the state Van Gorder dinners. Patrician to her finger tips, independent to the roots of her hair, she preserved, at 65, a humorous and quenchless curiosity in regard to every side of life, which even the full and crowded years that already lay behind her had not entirely satisfied. She was an Age and an Attitude, but she was more than that; she had grown old without growing dull or losing touch with youth—her face had the delicate strength of a fine cameo and her mild and youthful heart preserved an innocent zest for adventure.

Wide travel, social leadership, the world of art and books, a dozen charities, an existence rich with diverse experience—all these she had enjoyed energetically and to the full—but she felt, with ingenious vanity, that there were still sides to her character which even these had not brought to light. As a little girl she had hesitated between wishing to be a locomotive engineer or a famous bandit—and when she had found, at seven, that the accident of sex would probably debar her from either occupation, she had resolved fiercely that some time before she died she would show the world in general and the Van Gorder clan in particular that a woman was quite as capable of dangerous exploits as a man. So far her life, while exciting enough at moments, had never actually been dangerous and time was slipping away without giving her an opportunity to prove her hardiness of heart. Whenever she thought of this the fact annoyed her extremely—and she thought of it now.

She threw down the morning paper disgustedly. Here she was at 65—rich, safe, settled for the summer in a delightful country place with a good cook, excellent servants, beautiful gardens and grounds—everything as respectable and comfortable as—as a limousine! And out in the world people were murdering and robbing each other, floating over Niagara Falls in barrels, rescuing children from burning

21

houses, taming tigers, going to Africa to hunt gorillas, doing all sorts of exciting things! She could not float over Niagara Falls in a barrel; Lizzie Allen, her faithful old maid, would never let her! She could not go to Africa to hunt gorillas; Sally Ogden, her sister, would never let her hear the last of it. She could not even, as she certainly would if she were a man, try and track down this terrible creature, the Bat!

She sniffed disgruntedly. Things came to her much too easily. Take this very house she was living in. Ten days ago she had decided on the spur of the moment—a decision suddenly crystallized by a weariness of charitable committees and the noise and heat of New York—to take a place in the country for the summer. It was late in the renting season—even the ordinary difficulties of finding a suitable spot would have added some spice to the quest—but this ideal place had practically fallen into her lap, with no trouble or search at all. Courtleigh Fleming, president of the Union Bank, who had built the house on a scale of comfortable magnificence—Courtleigh Fleming had died suddenly in the West when Miss Van Gorder was beginning her house hunting. The day after his death her agent had called her up. Richard Fleming, Courtleigh Fleming's nephew and heir, was anxious to rent the Fleming house at once. If she made a quick decision it was hers for the summer, at a bargain. Miss Van Gorder had decided at once; she took an innocent pleasure in bargains.

And yet she could not really say that her move to the country had brought her no adventures at all. There had been—things. Last night the lights had

22

gone off unexpectedly and Billy, the Japanese butler and handy man, had said that he had seen a face at one of the kitchen windows — a face that vanished when he went to the window. Servants' nonsense, probably, but the servants seemed unusually nervous for people who were used to the country. And Lizzie, of course, had sworn that she had seen a man trying to get up the stairs but Lizzie could grow hysterical over a creaking door. Still — it was queer! And what had that affable Doctor Wells said to her — "I respect your courage, Miss Van Gorder — moving out into the Bat's home country, you know!" She picked up the paper again. There was a map of the scene of the Bat's most recent exploits and, yes, three of his recent crimes had been within a twenty-mile radius of this spot. She thought it over and gave a little shudder of pleasurable fear. Then she dismissed the thought with a shrug. No chance! She might live in a lonely house, two miles from the railroad station, all summer long — and the Bat would never disturb her. Nothing ever did.

She had skimmed through the paper hurriedly; now a headline caught her eye. *Failure of Union Bank* — wasn't that the bank of which Courtleigh Fleming had been president? She settled down to read the article but it was disappointingly brief. The Union Bank had closed its doors; the cashier, a young man named Bailey, was apparently under suspicion; the article mentioned Coutleigh Fleming's recent and tragic death in the best vein of newspaperese. She laid down the paper and thought — *Bailey — Bailey* — she seemed to have a vague recollection

23

of hearing about a young man named Bailey who worked in a bank — but she could not remember where or by whom his name had been mentioned.

Well, it didn't matter. She had other things to think about. She must ring for Lizzie, get up and dress. The bright morning sun, streaming in through the long window, made lying in bed an old woman's luxury and she refused to be an old woman.

Though the worst old woman I ever knew was a man, she thought with a satiric twinkle. She was glad Sally's daughter, young Dale Ogden, was here in the house with her. The companionship of Dale's bright youth would keep her from getting old-womanish if anything could.

She smiled, thinking of Dale. Dale was a nice child, her favorite niece. Sally didn't understand her, of course — but Sally wouldn't. Sally read magazine articles on the younger generation and its wild ways. *Sally doesn't remember when she was a younger generation herself,* thought Miss Cornelia. *But I do — and if we didn't have automobiles, we had buggies — and youth doesn't change its ways just because it has cut its hair.* Before Mr. and Mrs. Ogden left for Europe, Sally had talked to her sister Cornelia, long and weightily, on the problem of Dale. *Problem of Dale, indeed!* thought Miss Cornelia scornfully. *Dale's the nicest thing I've seen in some time. She'd be ten times happier if Sally wasn't always trying to marry her off to some young snip with more of what fools call 'eligibility' than brains! But there, Cornelia Van Gorder, Sally's given you your innings of rampaging off to Europe and leaving Dale*

24

with you all summer. You've a lot less sense than I flatter myself you have, if you can't give your favorite niece a happy vacation from all her immediate family and maybe find her someone who'll make her happy for good and all. Miss Cornelia was an incorrigible matchmaker.

Nevertheless, she was more concerned with "the problem of Dale" than she would have admitted. Dale, at her age, with her charm and beauty—*why, she ought to behave as if she were walking on air,* thought her aunt worriedly. *And instead she acts more as if she were walking on pins and needles. She seems to like being here, I know she likes me, I'm pretty sure she's just as pleased to get a little holiday from Sally and Harry. She amuses herself, she falls in with any plan I want to make, and yet*—And yet Dale was not happy; Miss Cornelia felt sure of it. *It isn't natural for a girl to seem so lackluster and—and quiet—at her age and she's nervous, too—as if something were preying on her mind, particularly these last few days. If she were in love with somebody, somebody Sally didn't approve of particularly—well, that would account for it, of course. But Sally didn't say anything that would make me think that—or Dale either—though I don't suppose Dale would, yet, even to me. I haven't seen so much of her in these last two years—*

Then Miss Cornelia's mind seized upon a sentence in a hurried flow of her sister's last instructions, a sentence that had passed almost unnoticed at the time, something about Dale and "an unfortunate attachment—but of course, Cornelia, dear she's so young—and I'm sure it will come to nothing now her father and I have made our attitude *plain!*"

Pshaw, I bet that's it, thought Miss Cornelia shrewdly. *Dale's fallen in love, or thinks she has, with some decent young man without a penny or an 'eligibility' to his name—and now she's unhappy because her parents don't approve—or because she's trying to give him up and finds she can't. Well—* and Miss Cornelia's tight little gray curls trembled with the vehemence of her decision, *if the young thing ever comes to me for advice I'll give her a piece of my mind that will surprise her and scandalize Sally Van Gorder Ogden out of her seven senses. Sally thinks nobody's worth looking at if they didn't come over to America when our family did.*

She was just stretching out her hand to ring for Lizzie when a knock came at the door. She gathered her Paisley shawl more tightly about her shoulders. "Who is it—oh, it's only you, Lizzie," as a pleasant Irish face, crowned by an old-fashioned pompadour of graying hair, peeped in at the door. "Good morning, Lizzie. I was just going to ring for you. Has Miss Dale had breakfast—I know it's shamefully late."

"Good morning, Miss Neily," said Lizzie, "and a lovely morning it is, too—if that was all of it," she added somewhat tartly as she came into the room with a little silver tray whereupon the morning mail reposed.

We have not yet described Lizzie Allen—and she deserves description. A fixture in the Van Gorder household since her sixteenth year, she had long ere now attained the dignity of a Tradition. The slip of a

26

colleen fresh from Kerry had grown old with her mistress, until the casual bond between mistress and servant had changed into something deeper; more in keeping with a better-mannered age than ours. One could not imagine Miss Cornelia without a Lizzie to grumble at and cherish—or Lizzie without a Miss Cornelia to baby and scold with the privileged frankness of such old family servitors. The two were at once a contrast and a complement. Fifty years of American ways had not shaken Lizzie's firm belief in banshees and leprechauns or tamed her wild Irish tongue; fifty years of Lizzie had not altered Miss Cornelia's attitude of fond exasperation with some of Lizzie's more startling eccentricities. Together they may have been, as one of the younger Van Gorder cousins had irreverently put it, "a scream," but apart each would have felt lost without the other.

"Now what do you mean—if that were all of it, Lizzie?" queried Miss Cornelia sharply as she took her letters from the tray.

Lizzie's face assumed an expression of doleful reticence.

"It's not my place to speak," she said with a grim shake of her head, "but I saw my grandmother last night, God rest her—plain as life she was, the way she looked when they waked her, and if it was *my* doing we'd be leaving this house this hour!"

"Cheese-pudding for supper—of course you saw your grandmother!" said Miss Cornelia crisply, slitting open the first of her letters with a paper knife. "Nonsense, Lizzie, I'm not going to be scared away from an ideal country place because you happen to

27

have a bad dream!"

"Was it a bad dream I saw on the stairs last night when the lights went out and I was looking for the candles?" said Lizzie heatedly. "Was it a bad dream that ran away from me and out the back door, as fast as Paddy's pig? No, Miss Neily, it was a man. Seven feet tall he was, and eyes that shone in the dark and—"

"Lizzie Allen!"

"Well, it's true for all that," insisted Lizzie stubbornly. "And why did the lights go out—tell me that, Miss Neily? They never go out in the city."

"Well, this isn't the city," said Miss Cornelia decisively. "It's the country, and very nice it is, and we're staying here all summer. I suppose I may be thankful," she went on ironically, "that it was only your grandmother you saw last night. It might have been the Bat—and then where would you be this morning?"

"I'd be stiff and stark with candles at me head and feet," said Lizzie gloomily. "Oh, Miss Neily, don't talk of that terrible creature, the Bat!" She came nearer to her mistress. *"There's bats in this house, too—real bats,"* she whispered impressively. "I saw one yesterday in the trunk room—the creature! It flew in the window and nearly had the switch off me before I could get away!"

Miss Cornelia chuckled. "Of course there are bats," she said. "There are always bats in the country. They're perfectly harmless, except to switches."

"And the Bat ye were talking of just then—he's harmless, too, I suppose?" said Lizzie with mournful satire. "Oh, Miss Neily, Miss Neily—do let's go back to the city before he flies away with us all!"

"Nonsense, Lizzie," said Miss Cornelia again, but this time less firmly. Her face grew serious. "If I thought for an instant that there was any real possibility of our being in danger here—" she said slowly. "But—oh, look at the map, Lizzie! The Bat has been—flying in this district—that's true enough but he hasn't come within ten miles of us yet!"

"What's ten miles to the Bat?" the obdurate Lizzie sighed. "And what of the letter ye had when ye first moved in here? *the Fleming house is unhealthy for strangers,* it said. *Leave it while ye can.*"

"Some silly boy or some crank." Miss Cornelia's voice was firm. "I never pay any attention to anonymous letters."

"And there's a funny-lookin' letter this mornin', down at the bottom of the pile—" persisted Lizzie. "It looked like the other one. I'd half a mind to throw it away before you saw it!"

"Now, Lizzie, that's quite enough!" Miss Cornelia had the Van Gorder manner on now. "I don't care to discuss your ridiculous fears any further. Where is Miss Dale?"

Lizzie assumed an attitude of prim rebuff. "Miss Dale's gone into the city, ma'am."

"Gone into the city?"

"Yes, ma'am. She got a telephone call this morning, early—long distance it was. I don't know who it was called her."

"Lizzie! You didn't listen?"

"Of course not, Miss Neily." Lizzie's face was a

study in injured virtue. "Miss Dale took the call in her own room and shut the door."

"And you were outside the door?"

"Where else would I be dustin' that time in the mornin'?" said Lizzie fiercely. "But it's yourself knows well enough the doors in this house is thick and not a sound goes past them."

"I should hope not," said Miss Cornelia rebukingly. "But tell me, Lizzie, did Miss Dale seem — well — this morning?"

"That she did not," said Lizzie promptly. "When she came down to breakfast, after the call, she looked like a ghost. I made her the eggs she likes, too — but she wouldn't eat 'em."

"H'm," Miss Cornelia pondered. "I'm sorry if — well, Lizzie, we mustn't meddle in Miss Dale's affairs."

"No, ma'am."

"But — did she say when she would be back?"

"Yes, Miss Neily. On the two o'clock train. Oh, and I was almost forgettin' — she told me to tell you particular — she said while she was in the city she'd be after engagin' the gardener you spoke of."

"The gardener? Oh, yes, I spoke to her about that the other night. The place is beginning to look run down — so many flowers to attend to. Well, that's very kind of Miss Dale."

"Yes, Miss Neily." Lizzie hesitated, obviously with some weighty news on her mind which she wished to impart. Finally she took the plunge. "I might have told Miss Dale she could have been lookin' for a cook as well — and a housemaid —" she muttered at last, "but they hadn't spoken to me then."

Miss Cornelia sat bolt upright in bed. "A cook—and a housemaid? But we have a cook and a housemaid, Lizzie! You don't mean to tell me—"

Lizzie nodded her head. "Yes'm. They're leaving. Both of 'em. Today."

"But good heav— Lizzie, why on earth didn't you tell me before?"

Lizzie spoke soothingly, all the blarney of Kerry in her voice. "Now, Miss Neily, as if I'd wake you first thing in the morning with bad news like that! And thinks I, well, maybe 'tis all for the best after all, for when Miss Neily hears they're leavin' and her so particular, maybe she'll go back to the city for just a little and leave this house to its haunts and its bats and—"

"Go back to the city? I shall do nothing of the sort. I rented this house to live in and live in it I will, with servants or without them. You should have told me at once, Lizzie. I'm really very much annoyed with you because you didn't. I shall get up immediately; I want to give those two a piece of my mind. Is Billy leaving too?"

"Not that I know of," said Lizzie sorrowfully, "And yet he'd be better riddance than cook or housemaid."

"Now, Lizzie, how many times have I told you that you must conquer your prejudices? Billy is an excellent butler. He'd been with Mr. Fleming ten years and has the very highest recommendations. I am very glad that he is staying, if he is. With you to help him, we shall do very well until I can get other servants."

31

Miss Cornelia had risen now and Lizzie was helping her with the intricacies of her toilet. "But it's too annoying," she went on, in the pauses of Lizzie's deft ministrations. "What did they say to you, Lizzie — did they give any reason? It isn't as if they were new to the country like you. They'd been with Mr. Fleming for some time, though not as long as Billy."

"Oh, yes, Miss Neily, they had reasons you could choke a goat with," said Lizzie viciously as she arranged Miss Cornelia's transformation. "Cook was the first of them — she was up late — I think they'd been talking it over together. She comes into the kitchen with her hat on and her bag in her hand. 'Good morning,' says I, pleasant enough, 'you've got your hat on,' says I. 'I'm leaving,' says she. 'Leaving, are you?' says I. 'Leaving,' says she. 'My sister has twins,' says she. 'I just got word, I must go to her right away.' 'What?' says I, all struck in a heap. 'Twins,' says she, 'you've heard of such things as twins.' 'That I have,' says I, 'and I know a lie on a face when I see it, too.' "

"Lizzie!"

"Well, it made me sick at heart, Miss Neily. Her with her hat and her bag and her talk about twins and no consideration for you. Well, I'll go on. 'You're a clever woman, aren't you?' says she — the impudence! 'I can see through a millstone as far as most,' says I. I wouldn't put up with her sauce. 'Well!' says she, 'you can see that Annie the house-maid's leaving, too.' 'Has her sister got twins as well?' says I and looked at her. 'No,' says she as bold as brass, 'but Annie's got a pain in her side and she's

32

feared it's appendycitis — so she's leaving to go back to her family.' 'Oh,' says I, 'and what about Miss Van Gorder?' 'I'm sorry for Miss Van Gorder,' says she — the falseness of her! — 'But she'll have to do the best she can for twins and appendycitis is acts of God and not to be put aside for even the best of wages.' 'Is that so?' says I and with that I left her, for I knew if I listened to her a minute longer I'd be giving her bonnet a shake and that wouldn't be respectable. So there you are, Miss Neily, and that's the gist of the matter."

Miss Cornelia laughed. "Lizzie, you're unique," she said. "But I'm glad you didn't give her bonnet a shake, though I've no doubt you could."

"Humph!" said Lizzie snorting, the fire of battle in her eye. "And is it any Black Irish from Ulster would play impudence to a Kerrywoman without getting the flat of a hand in, but that's neither here nor there. The truth of it is, Miss Neily," her voice grew solemn, "it's my belief they're scared, both of them, by the haunts and the banshees here — and that's all."

"If they are they're very silly," said Miss Cornelia practically. "No, they may have heard of a better place, though it would seem as if when one pays the present extortionate wages and asks as little as we do here — but it doesn't matter. If they want to go, they may. Am I ready, Lizzie?"

"You look like an angel, ma'am," said Lizzie, clasping her hands.

"Well, I feel very little like one," said Miss Cornelia, rising. "As cook and housemaid may discover before I'm through with them. Send them into the livingroom, Lizzie, when I've gone down. I'll talk to them there."

An hour or so later, Miss Cornelia sat in a deep chintz chair in the comfortable living-room of the Fleming house going through the pile of letters which Lizzie's news of domestic revolt had prevented her reading earlier. Cook and housemaid had come and gone—civil enough, but so obviously determined upon leaving the house at once that Miss Cornelia had sighed and let them go, though not without caustic comment. Since then, she had devoted herself to calling up various employment agencies without entirely satisfactory results. A new cook and house-maid were promised for the end of the week but for the next three days the Japanese butler, Billy, and Lizzie between them would have to bear the brunt of the service. *Oh, yes and then there's Dale's gardner, if she gets one,* thought Miss Cornelia. *I wish he could cook but I don't suppose gardeners can—and Billy's a treasure.*

She had reached the bottom of her pile of letters—these to be thrown away, these to be answered—ah, here was the one she had overlooked somehow. She took it up. It must be the one Lizzie had wanted to throw away; she smiled at Lizzie's fears. The address was badly typed, on cheap paper; she tore the envelope open and drew out a single unsigned sheet.

If you stay in this house any longer—DEATH. *Go back to the city at once and save your life.*

34

Her fingers trembled a little as she turned the missive over but her face remained calm. She looked at the envelope, at the postmark, while her heart thudded uncomfortably for a moment and then resumed its normal beat. It had come at last—the adventure—and she was not afraid!

Chapter Three: Pistol Practice

She knew who it was, of course. The Bat! No doubt of it. And yet—did the Bat ever threaten before he struck? She could not remember. But it didn't matter. The Bat was unprecedented—unique. At any rate, Bat or no Bat, she must think out a course of action. The defection of cook and housemaid left her alone in the house with Lizzie and Billy—and Dale, of course, if Dale returned. *Two old women, a young girl, and a Japanese butler to face the most dangerous criminal in America,* she thought grimly. And yet, one couldn't be sure. The threatening letter might be only a joke—a letter from a crank—after all. Still, she must take precautions; look for aid somewhere. But where could she look for aid?

She ran over in her mind the new acquaintances she had made since she moved to the country. There was Doctor Wells, the local physician, who had joked with her about moving into the Bat's home territory. He seemed an intelligent man but she knew him only slightly and she couldn't call a busy doctor away from his patients to investigate something which might only prove to be a mare's-nest.

The boys Dale had met at the country club—"Humph!" she sniffed, "I'd rather trust my gumption than any of theirs." The logical person to call on, of course, was Richard Fleming, Courtleigh Fleming's nephew and heir, who had rented her the house. He lived at the country club; she could probably reach him now. She was just on the point of doing so when she decided against it—partly from delicacy, partly from an indefinable feeling that he would not be of much help. *Besides,* she thought sturdily, *it's my house now, not his. He didn't guarantee burglar protection in the lease.*

As for the local police—her independence revolted at summoning them. They would bombard her with ponderous questions and undoubtedly think she was merely a nervous old spinster. *If it was just me,* she thought, *I swear I wouldn't say a word to anybody—and if the Bat flew in he mightn't find it so easy to fly out again, if I am sixty-five and never shot a burglar in my life! But there's Dale and Lizzie. I've got to be fair to them.*

For a moment she felt very helpless, very much alone. Then her courage returned.

"Pshaw, Cornelia, if you have got to get help—get the help *you* want and hang the consequences!" she adjured herself. "You've always hankered to see a first-class detective do his detecting—well, *get* one—or decide to do the job yourself. I'll bet you could at that."

She tiptoed to the main door of the living-room and closed it cautiously, smiling as she did so. Lizzie might be about and Lizzie would promptly go into hysterics if she got an inkling of her mistress's present intentions. Then she went to the city telephone and asked for long distance.

When she had finished her telephoning, she looked at once relieved and a little naughty—like a demure child who has carried out some piece of innocent mischief unobserved. "My stars!" she muttered to herself. "You never can tell what you can do till you try." Then she sat down again and tried to think of other measures of defense.

Now if I were the Bat, or any criminal, she mused, *how would I get into this house? Well, that's it—I might get in 'most any way—it's so big and rambling. All the grounds you want to lurk in, too; it'd take a company of police to shut them off. Then there's the house itself. Let's see—third floor—trunk room, servants' rooms—couldn't get in there very well except with a pretty long ladder—that's all right. Second floor—well, I suppose a man could get into my bedroom from the porch if I were an acrobat, but he'd need to be a very good acrobat and there's no use borrowing trouble. Downstairs is the problem, Cornelia, downstairs is the problem.*

"Take this room now." She rose and examined it carefully. "There's the door over there on the right that leads into the billiard room. There's this door over here that leads into the hall. Then there's that other door by the alcove, and all those French windows—whew!" She shook her head.

It was true. The room in which she stood, while comfortable and charming, seemed unusually accessible to the night prowler. A row of French windows at the rear gave upon a little terrace; below the terrace, the drive curved about and beneath the billiard-room windows in a hairpin loop, drawing up again at the main entrance on the other side of the house. At the left of the French windows (if one faced the terrace as Miss Cornelia was doing) was the alcove door of which she spoke. When open, it disclosed a little alcove, almost entirely devoted to the foot of a flight of stairs that gave direct access to the upper regions of the house. The alcove itself opened on one side upon the terrace and upon the other into a large butler's pantry. The arrangement was obviously designed so that, if necessary, one could pass directly from the terrace to the downstairs service quarters or the second floor of the house without going through the living-room, and so that trays could be carried up from the pantry by the side stairs without using the main staircase.

The middle pair of French windows were open, forming a double door. Miss Cornelia went over to them, shut them, tried the locks. *Humph! Flimsy enough!* she thought. Then she turned toward the billiard room.

The billiard room, as has been said, was the last room to the right in the main wing of the house. A single door led to it from the living-room. Miss Cornelia passed through this door, glanced about the billiard room, noting that most of its windows were too high from the ground to greatly encourage a marauder. She locked the only one that seemed to her particularly tempting — the billiard-room window on the terrace side of the house. Then she returned to the living-room and again considered her defenses.

Three points of access from the terrace to the house: the door that led into the alcove, the French windows of the living-room, the billiard-room window. On the other side of the house there was the main entrance, the porch, the library and dining-room windows. The main entrance led into a hall. The main door of the living-room was on the right as one entered, the dining-room and library on the left, the main staircase in front.

"My mind is starting to go round like a pinwheel, thinking of all those windows and doors," she murmured to herself. She sat down once more, and taking a pencil and a piece of paper drew a plan of the lower floor of the house.

And now I've studied it, she thought for a while, *I'm no further than if I hadn't. As far as I can figure out, there are so many ways for a clever man to get into this house that I'd have to be a couple of Siamese twins to watch it properly. The next house I rent in the country,* she decided, *just isn't going to have any windows and doors — or I'll know the reason why.*

But of course she was not entirely shut off from the world, even if the worst developed. She considered the telephone instruments on a table near the wall, one the general phone, the other connecting a house line which also connected with the garage and the greenhouses. The garage would not be helpful, since Slocum, her chauffeur for many years, had gone back to England for a visit. Dale had been driving the car. But with an able-bodied man in the gardener's house—

She pulled herself together with a jerk.

"Cornelia Van Gorder, you're going to go crazy before nightfall if you don't take hold of yourself. What you need is lunch and a nap in the afternoon if you can make yourself take it. You'd better look up that revolver of yours, too, that you bought when you thought you were going to take a trip to China. You've never fired it off yet, but you've got to sometime today; there's no other way of telling if it will work. You can shut your eyes when you do it—no, you can't either—that's silly.

"Call you a spirited old lady, do they? Well, you never had a better time to show your spirit than now!"

And Miss Van Gorder, sighing, left the living-room to reach the kitchen just in time to calm a heated argument between Lizzie and Billy on the relative merits of Japanese and Irish-American cooking.

Dale Ogden, taxiing up from the two o'clock train some time later, to her surprise discovered the front door locked and rang for some time before she could get an answer. At last, Billy appeared, white-coated, with an inscrutable expression on his face.

"Will you take my bag, Billy—thanks. Where is Miss Van Gorder—taking a nap?"

"No," said Billy succinctly. "She take no nap. She out in srubbery shotting."

Dale stared at him incredulously. "Shooting, Billy?"

"Yes, ma'am. At least—she not shott yet but she say she going to soon."

"But, good heavens, Billy—shooting what?"

"Shotting pistol," said Billy, his yellow mask of a face preserving its impish repose. He waved his hand. "You go srubbery. You see."

The scene that met Dale's eyes when she finally found the "srubbery" was indeed a singular one. Miss Van Gorder, her back firmly planted against the trunk of a large elm tree and an expression of ineffable distaste on her features, was holding out a blunt, deadly looking revolver at arm's length. Its muzzle wavered, now pointing at the ground, now at the sky. Behind the tree Lizzie sat in a heap, moaning quietly to herself, and now and then appealing to the saints to avert a visioned calamity.

As Dale approached, unseen, the climax came. The revolver steadied, pointed ferociously at an inoffensive grass-blade some 10 yards from Miss Van Gorder and went off. Lizzie promptly gave vent to a shrill Irish scream. Miss Van Gorder dropped the revolver like a hot potato and opened her mouth to tell Lizzie not to be such a fool. Then she saw Dale; her mouth went into a round O of horror and her hand clutched weakly at her heart.

"Good heavens, child!" she gasped. "Didn't Billy tell you what I was doing? I might have shot you like a rabbit!" and, overcome with emotion, she sat down on the ground and started to fan herself mechanically with a cartridge.

Dale couldn't help laughing, and the longer she looked at her aunt the more she laughed, until that dignified lady joined in the mirth herself.

"Aunt Cornelia, Aunt Cornelia!" said Dale when

she could get her breath. "That I've lived to see the day! Why on earth were you having pistol practice, darling—has Billy turned into a spy or what?"

Miss Van Gorder rose from the ground with as much stateliness as she could muster under the circumstances.

"No, my dear, but there's no fool like an old fool, that's all," she stated. "I've wanted to fire that infernal revolver off ever since I bought it two years ago, and now I have and I'm satisfied. Still," she went on thoughtfully, picking up the weapon, "it seems a very good revolver—and shooting people must be much easier than I supposed. All you have to do is to point the—the front of it—like this and—"

"Oh, Miss Dale, dear Miss Dale!" came the woebegone accents from the other side of the tree. "For the love of heaven, Miss Dale, say no more but take it away from her. She'll have herself all riddled through with bullets like a kitchen sieve, and me too, if she's let to have it again."

"Lizzie, I'm ashamed of you!" said Lizzie's mistress. "Come out from behind that tree and stop wailing like a siren. This weapon is perfectly safe in competent hands and—" She seemed on the verge of another demonstration of its powers.

"Miss Dale, for the dear love o' God, will you make her put it away?"

Dale laughed again. "I really think you'd better, Aunt Cornelia. Or both of us will have to put Lizzie to bed with a case of acute hysteria."

"Well," said Miss Van Gorder, "perhaps you're right, dear." Her eyes gleamed. "I *should* have liked to try it just once more though," she confided. "I feel certain that I could hit that tree over there if my eye wouldn't *wink* so when the thing goes off."

"Now, it's winking eyes," said Lizzie on a note of tragic chant, "but next time it'll be bleeding corpses and —"

Dale added her own protestations to Lizzie's. "Please, darling, if you really want to practice, Billy can fix up some sort of target range but I don't want my favorite aunt assassinated by a ricocheted bullet before my eyes!"

"Well, perhaps it would be best to try again another time," admitted Miss Van Gorder. But there was a wistful look in her eyes as she gave the revolver to Dale and the three started back to the house.

"I should *never* have allowed Lizzie to know what I was doing," she confided in a whisper, on the way. "A woman is perfectly capable of managing firearms — but Lizzie is really too nervous to live, sometimes."

"I know just how you feel, darling," Dale agreed, suppressed mirth shaking her as the little procession reached the terrace. "But — oh," she could keep it no longer, "oh — you did look funny, darling — sitting under that tree, with Lizzie on the other side of it making banshee noises and —"

Miss Van Gorder laughed too, a little shame-facedly.

"I must have," she said. "But — oh, you needn't shake your head, Lizzie Allen — I *am* going to practice with it. There's no reason I shouldn't and you never can tell when things like that might be useful," she ended rather vaguely. She did not wish to alarm

Dale with her suspicions yet.

"There, Dale—yes, put it in the drawer of the table—that will reassure Lizzie. Lizzie, you might make us some lemonade, I think—Miss Dale must be thirsty after her long, hot ride."

"Yes, Miss Cornelia," said Lizzie, recovering her normal calm as the revolver was shut away in the drawer of the large table in the living-room. But she could not resist one parting shot. "And thank God it's lemonade I'll be making—and not bandages for bullet wounds!" she muttered darkly as she went toward the service quarters.

Miss Van Gorder glared after her departing back. "Lizzie is really impossible sometimes!" she said with stately ire. Then her voice softened. "Though of course I couldn't do without her," she added.

Dale stretched out on the settee opposite her aunt's chair. "I know you couldn't, darling. Thanks for thinking of the lemonade." She passed her hand over her forehead in a gesture of fatigue. "I *am* hot—and tired."

Miss Van Gorder looked at her keenly. The young face seemed curiously worn and haggard in the clear afternoon light.

"You—you don't really feel very well, do you, Dale?"

"Oh—it's nothing. I feel all right—really."

"I could send for Doctor Wells if—"

"Oh, heavens, no, Aunt Cornelia." She managed a wan smile. "It isn't as bad as all that. I'm just tired and the city was terribly hot and noisy and—" She stole a glance at her aunt from between lowered lids.

45

"I got your gardener, by the way," she said casually.

"Did you, dear? That's splendid, though—but I'll tell you about that later. Where did you get him?"

"That good agency, I can't remember its name." Dale's hand moved restlessly over her eyes, as if remembering details were too great an effort. "But I'm sure he'll be satisfactory. He'll be out here this evening—he—he couldn't get away before, I believe. What have you been doing all day, darling?"

Miss Cornelia hesitated. Now that Dale had returned she suddenly wanted very much to talk over the various odd happenings of the day with her—get the support of her youth and her common sense. Then that independence which was so firmly rooted a characteristic of hers restrained her. No use worrying the child unnecessarily; they all might have to worry enough before tomorrow morning.

She compromised. "We have had a domestic upheaval," she said. "The cook and the housemaid have left; if you'd only waited till the next train you could have had the pleasure of their company into town."

"Aunt Cornelia, how exciting! I'm so sorry! Why did they leave?"

"Why do servants ever leave a good place?" asked Miss Cornelia grimly. "Because if they had sense enough to know when they were well off, they wouldn't be servants. Anyhow, they've gone; we'll have to depend on Lizzie and Billy the rest of this week. I telephoned—but they couldn't promise me any others before Monday."

"And I was in town and could have seen people for you—if I'd only known!" said Dale remorsefully.

46

"Only," she hesitated, "I mightn't have had time—at least I mean there were some other things I had to do, besides getting the gardener and—" She rose. "I think I will go and lie down for a little if you don't mind, darling."

Miss Van Gorder was concerned. "Of course I don't mind but—won't you even have your lemonade?"

"Oh, I'll get some from Lizzie in the pantry before I go up," Dale managed to laugh. "I think I must have a headache after all," she said. "Maybe I'll take an aspirin. Don't worry, darling."

"I shan't. I only wish there were something I could do for you, my dear."

Dale stopped in the alcove doorway. "There's nothing anybody can do for me, really," she said soberly. "At least—oh, I don't know what I'm saying! But don't worry. I'm quite all right. I may go over to the country club after dinner—and dance. Won't you come with me, Aunt Cornelia?"

"Depends on your escort," said Miss Cornelia tartly. "If our landlord, Mr. Richard Fleming, is taking you I certainly shall—I don't like his looks and never did!"

Dale laughed. "Oh, he's all right," she said. "Drinks a good deal and wastes a lot of money, but harmless enough. No, this is a very sedate party; I'll be home early."

"Well, in that case," said her aunt, "I shall stay here with my Lizzie and my ouija-board. Lizzie deserves *some* punishment for the *very* cowardly way she behaved this afternoon—and the ouija-board will

47

furnish it. She's scared to death to touch the thing. I think she believes it's alive."

"Well, maybe I'll send you a message on it from the country club," said Dale lightly. She had paused, halfway up the flight of side stairs in the alcove, and her aunt noticed how her shoulders drooped, belying the lightness of her voice. "Oh," she went on, "by the way — have the afternoon papers come yet? I didn't have time to get one when I was rushing for the train."

"I don't think so, dear, but I'll ask Lizzie." Miss Cornelia moved toward a bell push.

"Oh, don't bother; it doesn't matter. Only if they have, would you ask Lizzie to bring me one when she brings up the lemonade? I want to read about — about the Bat — he fascinates me."

"There was something else in the paper this morning," said Miss Cornelia idly. "Oh, yes — the Union Bank — the bank Mr. Fleming, Senior, was president of has failed. They seem to think the cashier robbed it. Did you see that, Dale?"

The shoulders of the girl on the staircase straightened suddenly. Then they drooped again. "Yes — I saw it," she said in a queerly colorless voice. "Too bad. It must be terrible to — to have everyone suspect you — and hunt you — as I suppose they're hunting that poor cashier."

"Well," said Miss Cornelia, "a man who wrecks a bank deserves very little sympathy to my way of thinking. But then I'm old-fashioned. Well, dear, I won't keep you. Run along and if you want an aspirin, there's a box in my top bureau-drawer."

48

"Thanks, darling. Maybe I'll take one and maybe I won't — all I really need is to lie down for a while."

She moved on up the staircase and disappeared from the range of Miss Cornelia's vision, leaving Miss Cornelia to ponder many things. Her trip to the city had done Dale no good, of a certainty. If not actually ill, she was obviously under some considerable mental strain. And why this sudden interest, first in the Bat, then in the failure of the Union Bank? Was it possible that Dale, too, had been receiving threatening letters?

I'll be glad when that gardener comes, she thought to herself. *He'll make a man in the house at any rate.*

When Lizzie at last came in with the lemonade she found her mistress shaking her head.

"Cornelia, Cornelia," she was murmuring to herself, "you should have taken to pistol practice when you were younger; it just shows how children waste their opportunities."

Chapter Four: The Storm Gathers

The long summer afternoon wore away, sunset came, red and angry, a sunset presaging storm. A chill crept into the air with the twilight. When night fell, it was not a night of silver patterns enskied, but a dark and cloudy cloak where a few stars glittered fitfully. Miss Cornelia, at dinner, saw a bat swoop past the window of the dining-room in its scurrying flight, and narrowly escaped oversetting her glass of water with a nervous start. The tension of waiting—waiting—for some vague menace which might not materialize after all—had begun to prey on her nerves. She saw Dale off to the country club with relief; the girl looked a little better after her nap but she was still not her normal self. When Dale was gone, she wandered restlessly for some time between living-room and library, now giving an unnecessary dusting to a piece of bric-a-brac with her handkerchief, now taking a book from one of the shelves in the library only to throw it down before she read a page.

This house was queer. She would not have admitted it to Lizzie, for her soul's salvation—but, for the first time in her sensible life, she listened for creakings of woodwork, rustling of leaves, stealthy steps outside, beyond the safe, bright squares of the windows—for anything that was actual, tangible, not merely formless fear.

"There's too much *room* in the country for things to happen to you!" she confided to herself with a shiver. "Even the night—whenever I look out, it seems to me as if the night were ten times bigger and blacker than it ever is in New York!"

To comfort herself she mentally rehearsed her telephone conversation of the morning, the conversation she had not mentioned to her household. At the time it had seemed to her most reassuring—the plans she had based upon it adequate and sensible in the normal light of day. But now the light of day had been blotted out and with it her security. Her plans seemed weapons of paper against the sinister might of the darkness beyond her windows.

She made herself sit down in the chair beside her favorite lamp on the center table and take up her knitting with stiff fingers. Knit two—purl two—Her hands fell into the accustomed rhythm mechanically. A spy, peering in through the French windows, would have deemed her the picture of calm. But she had never felt less calm in all the long years of her life.

She wouldn't ring for Lizzie to come and sit with her, she simply wouldn't. But she was very glad, nevertheless, when Lizzie appeared at the door.

"Miss Neily."

"Yes, Lizzie?" Miss Cornelia's voice was composed but her heart felt a throb of relief.

"Can I—can I sit in here with you, Miss Neily, just

51

a minute?" Lizzie's voice was plaintive. "I've been sitting out in the kitchen watching that Jap read his funny newspaper the wrong way and listening for ghosts till I'm nearly crazy!"

"Why, certainly, Lizzie," said Miss Cornelia primly. "Though," she added doubtfully, "I really shouldn't pamper your absurd fears, I suppose, but —"

"Oh, please, Miss Neily!"

"Very well," said Miss Cornelia brightly. "You can sit here, Lizzie — and help me work the ouija-board. That will take your mind off listening for things!"

Lizzie groaned. "You know I'd rather be shot than touch that uncanny ouijie!" she said dolefully. "It gives me the creeps every time I put my hands on it!"

"Well, of course, if you'd rather sit in the kitchen, Lizzie —"

"Oh, give me the ouijie!" said Lizzie in tones of heartbreak. "I'd rather be shot *and* stabbed than stay in the kitchen any more."

"Very well," said Miss Cornelia, "it's your own decision, Lizzie — remember that." Her needles clicked on. "I'll just finish this row before we start," she said "You might call up the light company in the meantime, Lizzie. There seems to be a storm coming up and I want to find out if they intend to turn out the lights tonight as they did last night. Tell them I find it most inconvenient to be left without light that way."

"It's worse than inconvenient," muttered Lizzie, "it's criminal, that's what it is, turning off all the lights in a haunted house like this one. As if spooks wasn't bad enough with the lights *on* —"

"Lizzie!"

"Yes, Miss Neily, I wasn't going to say another word." She went to the telephone. Miss Cornelia knitted on—knit two—purl two—In spite of her experiments with the ouija-board she didn't believe in ghosts, and yet, there were things one couldn't explain by logic. Was there something like that in this house—a shadow walking the corridors—a vague shape of evil, drifting like mist from room to room, till its cold breath whispered on one's back and—there! She had ruined her knitting, the last two rows would have to be ripped out. That came of mooning about ghosts like a ninny.

She put down the knitting with an exasperated little gesture. Lizzie had just finished her telephoning and was hanging up the receiver.

"Well, Lizzie?"

"Yes'm," said the latter, glaring at the phone. "That's what he says—they turned off the lights last night because there was a storm threatening. He says it burns out their fuses if they leave 'em on in a storm."

A louder roll of thunder punctuated her words.

"There!" said Lizzie. "They'll be going off again tonight." She took an uncertain step toward the French windows.

"Humph!" said Miss Cornelia, "I hope it will be a dry summer." Her hands tightened on each other. Darkness—darkness inside this house of whispers to match with the darkness outside! She forced herself to speak in a normal voice.

"Ask Billy to bring some candles, Lizzie—and have them ready."

Lizzie had been staring fixedly at the French windows. At Miss Cornelia's command she gave a little jump of terror and moved closer to her mistress.

"You're not going to ask me to go out in that hall alone?" she said in a hurt voice.

It was too much. Miss Cornelia found vent for her feelings in crisp exasperation.

"What's the matter with you anyhow, Lizzie Allen?"

The nervousness in her own tones infected Lizzie's. She shivered frankly.

"Oh, Miss Neily—Miss Neily!" she pleaded. "I don't like it! I want to go back to the city!"

Miss Cornelia braced herself. "I have rented this house for four months and I am going to stay," she said firmly. Her eyes sought Lizzie's, striving to pour some of her own inflexible courage into the latter's quaking form. But Lizzie would not look at her. Suddenly she started and gave a low scream.

"There's somebody on the terrace!" she breathed in a ghastly whisper, clutching at Miss Cornelia's arm.

For a second Miss Cornelia sat frozen. Then, "Don't do that!" she said sharply. "What nonsense!" but she looked over her shoulder as she said it and Lizzie saw the look. Both waited, in pulsing stillness—one second—two.

"I guess it was the wind," said Lizzie at last, relieved, her grip on Miss Cornelia relaxing. She began to look a trifle ashamed of herself and Miss Cornelia seized the opportunity.

"You were born on a brick pavement," she said crushingly. "You get nervous out here at night whenever a cricket begins to sing—or scrape his legs—or whatever it is they do!"

54

Lizzie bowed before the blast of her mistress's scorn and began to move gingerly toward the alcove door. But obviously she was not entirely convinced.

"Oh, it's more than that, Miss Neily," she mumbled. "I—"

Miss Cornelia turned to her fiercely. If Lizzie was going to behave like this, they might as well have it out now between them—before Dale came home.

"What did you *really* see last night?" she said in a minatory voice.

The instant relief on Lizzie's face was ludicrous; she so obviously preferred discussing any subject at any length to braving the dangers of the other part of the house unaccompanied.

"I was standing right there at the top of that there staircase," she began, gesticulating toward the alcove stairs in the manner of one who embarks upon the narration of an epic. "Standing there with your switch in my hand, Miss Neily—and then I looked down and," her voice dropped. "I saw a *gleaming eye!* It looked at me and *winked!* I tell you this house is haunted!"

"A flirtatious ghost?" queried Miss Cornelia skeptically. She snorted. "Humph! Why didn't you yell?"

"I was too scared to yell! And I'm not the only one." She started to back away from the alcove, her eyes still fixed upon its haunted stairs. "Why do you think the servants left so sudden this morning?" she went on. "Do you really believe the housemaid had appendicitis? Or the cook's sister had twins?"

She turned and gestured at her mistress with a long, pointed forefinger. Her voice had a note of doom.

55

"I bet a cent the cook never had any sister—and the sister never had any twins," she said impressively. "No, Miss Neily, they couldn't put it over on me like that! They were scared away. They saw—It!"

She concluded her epic and stood nodding her head, an Irish Cassandra who had prophesied the evil to come.

"Fiddlesticks!" said Miss Cornelia briskly, more shaken by the recital than she would have admitted. She tried to think of another topic of conversation.

"What time is it?" she asked.

Lizzie glanced at the mantel clock. "Half-past ten, Miss Neily."

Miss Cornelia yawned, a little dismally. She felt as if the last two hours had not been hours but years.

"Miss Dale won't be home for half an hour," she said reflectively. *And if I have to spend another thirty minutes listening to Lizzie shiver,* she thought, *Dale will find me a nervous wreck when she does come home.* She rolled up her knitting and put it back in her knitting-bag; it was no use going on, doing work that would have to be ripped out again and yet she must do something to occupy her thoughts. She raised her head and discovered Lizzie returning toward the alcove stairs with the stealthy tread of a panther. The sight exasperated her.

"Now, Lizzie Allen!" she said sharply, "you forget all that superstitious nonsense and stop looking for ghosts! There's nothing in that sort of thing." She smiled—she would punish Lizzie for her obdurate timorousness. "Where's that ouija-board?" she questioned, rising, with determination in her eye.

Lizzie shuddered violently. "It's up there—with a

56

prayer book on it to keep it quiet!" she groaned, jerking her thumb in the direction of the farther bookcase.

"Bring it here!" said Miss Cornelia implacably; then as Lizzie still hesitated, "Lizzie!"

Shivering, every movement of her body a conscious protest, Lizzie slowly went over to the bookcase, lifted off the prayer book, and took down the ouija-board. Even then she would not carry it normally but bore it over to Miss Cornelia at arms'-length, as if any closer contact would blast her with lightning, her face a comic mask of loathing and repulsion.

She placed the lettered board in Miss Cornelia's lap with a sigh of relief. "You can do it yourself! I'll have none of it!" she said firmly.

"It takes two people and you know it, Lizzie Allen!" Miss Cornelia's voice was stern but it was also amused.

Lizzie groaned, but she knew her mistress. She obeyed. She carefully chose the farthest chair in the room and took a long time bringing it over to where her mistress sat waiting.

"I've been working for you for twenty years," she muttered. "I've been your goat for twenty years and I've got a right to speak my mind—"

Miss Cornelia cut her off. "You haven't got a mind. Sit down," she commanded.

Lizzie sat, her hands at her sides. With a sigh of tried patience, Miss Cornelia put her unwilling fingers on the little moving table that is used to point to the letters on the board itself. Then she placed her own hands on it, too, the tips of the fingers just

57

touching Lizzie's.

"Now make your mind a blank!" she commanded her factotum.

"You just said I haven't got any mind," complained the latter.

"Well," said Miss Cornelia magnificently, "make what you haven't got a blank."

The repartee silenced Lizzie for the moment, but only for the moment. As soon as Miss Cornelia had settled herself comfortably and tried to make her mind a suitable receiving station for ouija messages, Lizzie began to mumble the sorrows of her heart.

"I've stood by you through thick and thin," she mourned in a low voice. "I stood by you when you were a vegetarian, I stood by you when you were a theosophist, and I seen you through socialism, Fletcherism and rheumatism—but when it comes to carrying on with ghosts—"

"Be still!" ordered Miss Cornelia. "Nothing will come if you keep chattering!"

"That's *why* I'm chattering!" said Lizzie, driven to the wall. "My teeth are, too," she added. "I can hardly keep my upper set in," and a desolate clicking of artificial molars attested the truth of the remark. Then, to Miss Cornelia's relief, she was silent for nearly two minutes, only to start so violently at the end of the time that she nearly upset the ouija-board on her mistress's toes.

"I've got a queer feeling in my fingers—all the way up my arms," she whispered in awed accents, wriggling the arms she spoke of violently.

"Hush!" said Miss Cornelia indignantly. Lizzie always exaggerated, of course—yet now her own fingers felt prickly, uncanny. There was a little pause while both sat tense, staring at the board.

"Now, Ouija," said Miss Cornelia defiantly, "is Lizzie Allen right about this house or is it all stuff and nonsense?"

For one second—two—the ouija remained anchored to its resting place in the center of the board. Then—

"My Gawd! It's moving!" said Lizzie in tones of pure horror as the little pointer began to wander among the letters.

"You shoved it!"

"I did not. Cross my heart, Miss Neily—I—" Lizzie's eyes were round, her fingers glued rigidly and awkwardly to the ouija. As the movements of the pointer grew more rapid her mouth dropped open, wider and wider, prepared for an ear-piercing scream.

"Keep quiet!" said Miss Cornelia tensely. There was a pause of a few seconds while the pointer darted from one letter to another wildly.

"B—M—C—X—P—R—S—K—Z—" murmured Miss Cornelia trying to follow the spelled letters.

"It's Russian!" gasped Lizzie breathlessly and Miss Cornelia nearly disgraced herself in the eyes of any spirits that might be present by inappropriate laughter. The ouija continued to move—more letters—what was it spelling?—it couldn't be—good heavens—

"B—A—T—Bat!" said Miss Cornelia with a tiny catch in her voice.

The pointer stopped moving. She took her hands from the board.

"That's queer," she said with a forced laugh. She

glanced at Lizzie to see how Lizzie was taking it. But the latter seemed too relieved to have her hands off the ouija-board to make the mental connection that her mistress had feared.

All she said was, "Bats indeed! That shows it's spirits. There's been a bat flying around this house all evening."

She got up from her chair tentatively, obviously hoping that the séance was over.

"Oh, Miss Neily," she burst out. "Please let me sleep in your room tonight! It's only when my jaw drops that I snore, I can tie it up with a handkerchief!"

"I wish you'd tie it up with a handkerchief now," said her mistress absent-mindedly, still pondering the message that the pointer had spelled. "B — A — T — Bat!" she murmured. Thought transference — warning — accident? Whatever it was, it was — nerve shaking. She put the ouija-board aside. Accident or not, she was done with it for the evening. But she could not so easily dispose of the Bat. Sending a protesting Lizzie off for her reading glasses, Miss Cornelia got the evening paper and settled down to what by now had become her obsession. She had not far to search for a long black streamer ran across the front page — *Bat Baffles Police Again*.

She skimmed through the article with eerie fascination, reading bits of it aloud for Lizzie's benefit.

" 'Unique criminal — long baffled the police — record of his crimes shows him to be endowed with an almost diabolical ingenuity — so far there is no clue to his identity — ' " *Pleasant reading for an old woman who's just received a threatening letter,* she thought ironically—ah, here was something new in a black-bordered box on the front page—a statement by the paper.

She read it aloud. " 'We must cease combing the criminal world for the Bat and look higher. He may be a merchant—a lawyer—a doctor—honored in his community by day and at night a bloodthirsty assassin—' " The print blurred before her eyes, she could read no more for the moment. She thought of the revolver in the drawer of the table close at hand and felt glad that it was there, loaded.

"I'm going to take the butcher knife to bed with me!" Lizzie was saying.

Miss Cornelia touched the ouija-board. "That thing certainly spelled Bat," she remarked. "I wish I were a man. I'd like to see any lawyer, doctor, or merchant of my acquaintance leading a double life without my suspecting it."

"Every man leads a double life and some more than that," Lizzie observed. "I guess it rests them, like it does me to take off my corset."

Miss Cornelia opened her mouth to rebuke her but just at that moment there was a clink of ice from the hall, and Billy, the Japanese, entered carrying a tray with a pitcher of water and some glasses on it. Miss Cornelia watched his impassive progress, wondering if the Oriental races ever felt terror; she could not imagine all Lizzie's banshees and kelpies producing a single shiver from Billy. He set down the tray and was about to go as silently as he had come when Miss Cornelia spoke to him on impulse.

"Billy, what's all this about the cook's sister not having twins?" she said in an offhand voice. She had

61

not really discussed the departure of the other servants with Billy before. "Did you happen to know that this interesting event was anticipated?"

Billy drew in his breath with a polite hiss. "Maybe she have twins," he admitted. "It happen sometime. Mostly not expected."

"Do you think there was any other reason for her leaving?"

"Maybe," said Billy blandly.

"Well, what was the reason?"

"All say the same thing—house haunted." Billy's reply was prompt as it was calm.

Miss Cornelia gave a slight laugh. "You know better than that, though, don't you?"

Billy's Oriental placidity remained unruffled. He neither admitted nor denied. He shrugged his shoulders.

"Funny house," he said laconically. "Find window open—nobody there. Door slam—nobody there!"

On the heels of his words came a single, startling bang from the kitchen quarters—the bang of a slammed door!

Chapter Five: Alopecia and Rubeola

Miss Cornelia dropped her newspaper. Lizzie, frankly frightened, gave a little squeal and moved closer to her mistress. Only Billy remained impassive but even he looked sharply in the direction whence the sound had come.

Miss Cornelia was the first of the others to recover her poise.

"Stop that! It was the wind!" she said, a little irritably—the "Stop that!" addressed to Lizzie who seemed on the point of squealing again.

"I think not wind," said Billy. His very lack of perturbation added weight to the statement. It made Miss Cornelia uneasy. She took out her knitting again.

"How long have you lived in this house, Billy?"

"Since Mr. Fleming built."

"H'm." Miss Cornelia pondered. "And this is the first time you have been disturbed?"

"Last two days only." Billy would have made an ideal witness in a courtroom. He restricted himself so precisely to answering what was asked of him in as few words as possible.

"What about that face Lizzie said you saw last night at the window?" she asked in a steady voice.

Billy grinned, as if slightly embarrassed.

"Just face—that's all."

"A—man's face?"

He shrugged again.

"Don't know—maybe. It there! It gone!"

Miss Cornelia did not want to believe him—but she did. "Did you go out after it?" she persisted.

Billy's yellow grin grew wider. "No thanks," he said cheerfully with ideal succinctness.

Lizzie, meanwhile, had stood first on one foot and then on the other during the interrogation, terror and morbid interest fighting in her for mastery. Now she could hold herself in no longer.

"Oh, Miss Neily!" she exploded in a graveyard moan, "last night when the lights went out I had a token! My oil lamp was full of oil but, do what I would, it kept going out, too—the minute I shut my eyes, out that lamp would go. There ain't a surer token of death! The Bible says, 'Let your light shine'—and when a hand you can't see puts your lights out—good night!"

She ended in a hushed whisper and even Billy looked a trifle uncomfortable after her climax.

"Well, now that you've cheered us up," began Miss Cornelia undauntedly, but a long, ominous roll of thunder that rattled the panes in the French windows drowned out the end of her sentence. Nevertheless she welcomed the thunder as a diversion. At least its menace was a physical one, to be guarded against by

64

physical means.

She rose and went over to the French windows. That flimsy bolt! She parted the curtains, and looked out; a flicker of lightning stabbed the night, the storm must be almost upon them.

"Bring some candles, Billy," she said. "The lights may be going out any moment—and Billy," as he started to leave, "there's a gentleman arriving on the last train. After he comes you may go to bed. I'll wait up for Miss Dale—oh, and Billy," arresting him at the door, "see that all the outer doors on this floor are locked and bring the keys here."

Billy nodded and departed. Miss Cornelia took a long breath. Now that the moment for waiting had passed, the moment for action come—she felt suddenly indomitable, prepared to face a dozen Bats!

Her feelings were not shared by her maid. "I know what all this means," moaned Lizzie. "I tell you there's going to be a death, sure!"

"There certainly will be if you don't keep quiet," said her mistress acidly. "Lock the billiard-room windows and go to bed."

But this was the last straw for Lizzie. A picture of the two long, dark flights of stairs up which she had to pass to reach her bedchamber rose before her—and she spoke her mind.

"I am not going to bed!" she said wildly. "I'm going to pack up tomorrow and leave this house." That such a threat would never be carried out while she lived made little difference to her, she was beyond the need of Truth's consolations. "I asked you on my bended knees not to take this place two miles from a

65

railroad," she went on heatedly. "For mercy's sake, Miss Neily, let's go back to the city before it's too late!"

Miss Cornelia was inflexible.

"I'm not going. You can make up your mind to that. I'm going to find out what's wrong with this place if it takes all summer. I came out to the country for a rest and I'm going to *get* it."

"You'll get your heavenly rest!" mourned Lizzie, giving it up. She looked pitifully at her mistress's face for a sign that the latter might be weakening but no such sign came. Instead, Miss Cornelia seemed to grow more determined.

"Besides," she said, suddenly deciding to share the secret she had hugged to herself all day, "I might as well tell you, Lizzie. I'm having a detective sent down tonight from police headquarters in the city."

"A detective?" Lizzie's face was horrified. "Miss Neily, you're keeping something from me! You know something I don't know."

"I hope so. I daresay he will be stupid enough. Most of them are. But at least we can have one proper night's sleep."

"Not I. I trust no man," said Lizzie. But Miss Cornelia had picked up the paper again.

" 'The Bat's last crime was a particularly atrocious one,' " she read. " 'The body of the murdered man—' "

But Lizzie could bear no more.

"Why don't you read the funny page once in a while?" she wailed and hurried to close the windows in the billiard room. The door leading into the bil-

66

liard room shut behind her.

Miss Cornelia remained reading for a moment. Then — was that a sound from the alcove? She dropped the paper, went into the alcove and stood for a moment at the foot of the stairs, listening. No — it must have been imagination. But, while she was here, she might as well put on the spring lock that bolted the door from the alcove to the terrace. She did so, returned to the living-room and switched off the lights for a moment to look out at the coming storm. It was closer now — the lightning flashes more continuous. She turned on the lights again as Billy re-entered with three candles and a box of matches.

He put them down on a side table.

"New gardener come," he said briefly to Miss Cornelia's back.

Miss Cornelia turned. "Nice hour for him to get here. What's his name?"

"Say his name Brook," said Billy, a little doubtful. English names still bothered him — he was never quite sure of them at first.

Miss Cornelia thought. "Ask him to come in," she said. "And Billy — where are the keys?"

Billy silently took two keys from his pocket and laid them on the table. Then he pointed to the terrace door which Miss Cornelia had just bolted.

"Door up there — spring lock," he said.

"Yes." She nodded. "And the new bolt you put on today makes it fairly secure. One thing is fairly sure, Billy. If anyone tries to get in tonight, he will have to break a window and make a certain amount of noise."

But he only smiled his curious enigmatic smile and went out. And no sooner had Miss Cornelia seated herself when the door of the billiard room slammed open suddenly and Lizzie burst into the room as if she had been shot from a gun—her hair wild—her face stricken with fear.

"I heard somebody yell out in the grounds—away down by the gate!" she informed her mistress in a loud stage whisper which had a curious note of pride in it, as if she were not too displeased at seeing her doleful predictions so swiftly coming to pass.

Miss Cornelia took her by the shoulder—half-startled, half-dubious.

"What did they yell?"

"Just yelled a yell!"

"Lizzie!"

"I heard them!"

But she had cried "Wolf!" too often.

"You take a liver pill," said her mistress disgustedly, "and go to bed."

Lizzie was about to protest both the verdict on her story and the judgment on herself when the door in the hall was opened by Billy to admit the new gardener. A handsome young fellow, in his late twenties, he came two steps into the room and then stood there respectfully with his cap in his hand, waiting for Miss Cornelia to speak to him.

After a swift glance of observation that gave her food for thought she did so.

"You are Brooks, the new gardener?"

The young man inclined his head.

"Yes, madam. The butler said you wanted to speak

to me."

Miss Cornelia regarded him anew. *His hands look soft—for a gardener's,* she thought. *And his manners seem much too good for one—still—*

"Come in," she said briskly. The young man advanced another two steps. "You're the man my niece engaged in the city this afternoon?"

"Yes, madam." He seemed a little uneasy under her searching scrutiny. She dropped her eyes.

"I could not verify your references as the Brays are in Canada—" she proceeded.

The young man took an eager step forward. "I am sure if Mrs. Bray were here—" he began, then flushed and stopped, twisting his cap.

"*Were* here?" said Miss Cornelia in a curious voice. "Are you a *professional* gardener?"

"Yes." The young man's manner had grown a trifle defiant but Miss Cornelia's next question followed remorselessly.

"Know anything about hardy perennials?" she said in a soothing voice, while Lizzie regarded the interview with wondering eyes.

"Oh, yes," but the young man seemed curiously lacking in confidence. "They—they're the ones that keep their leaves during the winter, aren't they?"

"Come over here—closer—" said Miss Cornelia imperiously. Once more she scrutinized him and this time there was no doubt of his discomfort under her stare.

"Have you had any experience with ruboela?" she queried finally.

"Oh, yes—yes—yes, indeed," the gardener stammered. "Yes."

"And—alopecia?" pursued Miss Cornelia.

The young man seemed to fumble in his mind for the characteristics of such a flower or shrub.

"The dry weather is very hard on alopecia," he asserted finally, and was evidently relieved to see Miss Cornelia receive the statement with a pleasant smile.

"What do you think is the best treatment for urticaria?" she propounded with a highly professional manner.

It appeared to be a catch-question. The young man knotted his brows. Finally a gleam of light seemed to come to him.

"Urticaria frequently needs—er—thinning," he announced decisively.

"Needs scratching you mean!" Miss Cornelia rose with a snort of disdain and faced him. "Young man, urticaria is *hives,* rubeola is *measles,* and alopecia is *baldness!*" she thundered. She waited a moment for his defense. None came.

"Why did you tell me you were a professional gardener?" she went on accusingly. "Why have you come here at this hour of night pretending to be something you're not?"

By all standards of drama the young man should have wilted before her wrath. Instead he suddenly smiled at her, boyishly, and threw up his hands in a gesture of defeat.

"I know I shouldn't have done it!" he confessed with appealing frankness. "You'd have found me out anyhow! I don't know anything about gardening. The truth is," his tone grew somber, "I was desperate!

I had to have work!"

The candor of his smile would have disarmed a stonier-hearted person than Miss Cornelia. But her suspicions were still awake.

"That's all, is it?"

"That's enough when you're down and out." His words had an unmistakable accent of finality. She couldn't help wanting to believe him, and yet, he wasn't what he had pretended to be—and this night of all nights was no time to take people on trust!

"How do I know you won't steal the spoons?" she queried, her voice still gruff.

"Are they nice spoons?" he asked with absurd seriousness.

She couldn't help smiling at his tone. "Beautiful spoons."

Again that engaging, boyish manner of his touched something in her heart.

"Spoons are a great temptation to me, Miss Van Gorder, but if you'll take me, I'll promise to leave them alone."

"That's extremely kind of you," she answered with grim humor, knowing herself beaten. She went over to ring for Billy.

Lizzie took the opportunity to gain her ear.

"I don't trust him, Miss Neily! He's too smooth!" she whispered warningly.

Miss Cornelia stiffened. "I haven't asked for your opinion, Lizzie," she said.

But Lizzie was not to be put off by the Van Gorder manner.

"Oh," she whispered, "you're just as bad as all the

71

rest of 'em. A good-looking man comes in the door and your brains fly out the window!"

Miss Cornelia quelled her with a gesture and turned back to the young man. He was standing just where she had left him, his cap in his hands—but, while her back had been turned, his eyes had made a stealthy survey of the living-room—a survey that would have made it plain to Miss Cornelia, if she had seen him, that his interest in the Fleming establishment was not merely the casual interest of a servant and his new place of abode. But she had not seen and she could have told nothing from his present expression.

"Have you had anything to eat lately?" she asked in a kindly voice.

He looked down at his cap. "Not since this morning," he admitted as Billy answered the bell.

Miss Cornelia turned to the impassive Japanese.

"Billy, give this man something to eat and then show him where he is to sleep."

She hesitated. The gardener's house was some distance from the main building, and with the night and the approaching storm she felt her own courage weakening. Into the bargain, whether this stranger had lied about his gardening or not, she was curiously attracted to him.

"I think," she said slowly, "that I'll have you sleep in the house here, at least for tonight. Tomorrow we can—the housemaid's room, Billy," she told the butler. And before their departure she held out a candle and a box of matches.

"Better take these with you, Brooks," she said.

"The local light company crawls under its bed every time there is a thunderstorm. Good night, Brooks."

"Good night, ma'am," said the young man smiling. Following Billy to the door, he paused. "You're being mighty good to me," he said diffidently, smiled again, and disappeared after Billy.

As the door closed behind them, Miss Cornelia found herself smiling too. "That's a pleasant young fellow—no matter what he is," she said to herself decidedly, and not even Lizzie's feverish "Haven't you any sense taking strange men into the house? How do you know he isn't the Bat?" could draw a reply from her.

Again the thunder rolled as she straightened the papers and magazines on the table and Lizzie gingerly took up the ouija-board to replace it on the bookcase with the prayer book firmly on top of it. And this time, with the roll of the thunder, the lights in the living-room blinked uncertainly for an instant before they recovered their normal brilliance.

"There go the lights!" grumbled Lizzie, her fingers still touching the prayer book, as if for protection. Miss Cornelia did not answer her directly.

"We'll put the detective in the blue room when he comes," she said. "You'd better go up and see if it's all ready."

Lizzie started to obey, going toward the alcove to ascend to the second floor by the alcove stairs. But Miss Cornelia stopped her.

"Lizzie—you know that stair rail's just been varnished. Miss Dale got a stain on her sleeve there this afternoon—and Lizzie—"

"Yes'm?"

"No one is to know that he is a detective. Not even Billy." Miss Cornelia was very firm.

"Well, what'll I *say* he is?"

"It's nobody's business."

"A detective," moaned Lizzie, opening the hall door to go by the main staircase. "Tiptoeing around with his eye to all the keyholes. A body won't be safe in the bathtub." She shut the door with a little slap and disappeared. Miss Cornelia sat down—she had many things to think over. *If I ever get time really to think of anything again,* she thought, *because with gardeners coming who aren't gardeners—and Lizzie hearing yells in the grounds and—*

She started slightly. The front door bell was ringing—a long trill, uncannily loud in the quiet house.

She sat rigid in her chair, waiting. Billy came in.

"Front door key, please?" he asked urbanely. She gave him the key.

"Find out who it is before you unlock the door," she said. He nodded. She heard him at the door, then a murmur of voices—Dale's voice and another's—"Won't you come in for a few minutes?" "Oh, thank you." She relaxed.

The door opened; it was Dale. *How lovely she looks in that evening wrap!* thought Miss Cornelia. *But how tired, too. I wish I knew what was worrying her.*

She smiled. "Aren't you back early, Dale?"

Dale threw off her wrap and stood for a moment patting back into its becoming coiffure, hair ruffled by the wind.

74

"I was tired," she said, sinking into a chair.

"Not worried about anything?" Miss Cornelia's eyes were sharp.

"No," said Dale without conviction, "but I've come here to be company for you and I don't want to run away all the time." She picked up the evening paper and looked at it without apparently seeing it. Miss Cornelia heard voices in the hall—a man's voice—affable—"How have you been, Billy?"—Billy's voice in answer, "Very well, sir."

"Who's out there, Dale?" she queried.

Dale looked up from the paper. "Doctor Wells, darling," she said in a listless voice. "He brought me over from the club; I asked him to come in for a few minutes. Billy's just taking his coat." She rose, threw the paper aside, came over and kissed Miss Cornelia suddenly and passionately—then, before Miss Cornelia, a little startled, could return the kiss, went over and sat on the settee by the fireplace near the door of the billiard room.

Miss Cornelia turned to her with a thousand questions on her tongue, but before she could ask any of them, Billy was ushering in Doctor Wells.

As she shook hands with the doctor, Miss Cornelia observed him with casual interest—wondering why such a good-looking man, in his early forties, apparently built for success, should be content with the comparative rustication of his local practice. That shrewd, rather aquiline face, with its keen gray eyes, would have found itself more at home in a wider sphere of action, she thought—there was just that touch of ruthlessness about it which makes or mars a captain in the world's affairs. She found herself murmuring the usual conventionalities of greeting.

"Oh, I'm very well, Doctor, thank you. Well, many people at the country club?"

"Not very many," he said, with a shake of his head. "This failure of the Union Bank has knocked a good many of the club members sky high."

"Just how did it happen?" Miss Cornelia was making conversation.

"Oh, the usual thing." The doctor took out his cigarette case. "The cashier, a young chap named Bailey, looted the bank to the tune of over a million."

Dale turned sharply toward them from her seat by the fireplace.

"How do you *know* the cashier did it?" she said in a low voice.

The doctor laughed. "Well—he's run away, for one thing. The bank examiners found the deficit. Bailey, the cashier, went out on an errand and didn't come back. The method was simple enough—worthless bonds substituted for good ones—with a good bond on the top and bottom of each package, so the packages would pass a casual inspection. Probably been going on for some time."

The fingers of Dale's right hand drummed restlessly on the edge of her settee.

"Couldn't somebody else have done it?" she queried tensely.

The doctor smiled, a trifle patronizingly.

"Of course the president of the bank had access to the vaults," he said. "But, as you know, Mr. Courtleigh Fleming, the late president, was buried

76

last Monday."

Miss Cornelia had seen her niece's face light up oddly at the beginning of the doctor's statement—to relapse into lassitude again at its conclusion. Bailey—Bailey—she was sure she remembered that name—on Dale's lips.

"Dale, dear, did you know this young Bailey?" she asked point-blank.

The girl had started to light a cigarette. The flame wavered in her fingers, the match went out.

"Yes—slightly," she said. She bent to strike another match, averting her face. Miss Cornelia did not press her.

"What with bank robberies and communism and the income tax," she said, turning the subject, "the only way to keep your money these days is to spend it."

"Or not to have any—like myself!" the doctor agreed.

"It seems strange," Miss Cornelia went on, "living in Courtleigh Fleming's house. A month ago I'd never even heard of Mr. Fleming, though I suppose I should have, and now—why, I'm as interested in the failure of his bank as if I were a depositor!"

The doctor regarded the end of his cigarette.

"As a matter of fact," he said pleasantly, "Dick Fleming had no right to rent you the property before the estate was settled. He must have done it the moment he received my telegram announcing his uncle's death."

"Were you with him when he died?"

"Yes, in Colorado. He had angina pectoris and

took me with him for that reason. But with care he might have lived a considerable time. The trouble was that he wouldn't use ordinary care. He ate and drank more than he should, and so—"

"I suppose," pursued Miss Cornelia, watching Dale out of the corner of her eye, "that there is no suspicion that Courtleigh Fleming robbed his own bank?"

"Well, if he did," said the doctor amicably, "I can testify that he didn't have the loot with him." His tone grew more serious. "No! He had his faults—but not that."

Miss Cornelia made up her mind. She had resolved before not to summon the doctor for aid in her difficulties, but now that chance had brought him here the opportunity seemed too good a one to let slip.

"Doctor," she said, "I think I ought to tell you something. Last night and the night before, attempts were made to enter this house. Once an intruder actually got in and was frightened away by Lizzie at the top of that staircase." She indicated the alcove stairs. "And twice I have received anonymous communications threatening my life if I did not leave the house and go back to the city."

Dale rose from her settee, startled.

"I didn't know that, Auntie! How dreadful!" she gasped.

Instantly Miss Cornelia regretted her impulse of confidence. She tried to pass the matter off with tart humor.

"Don't tell Lizzie," she said. "She'd yell like a siren. It's the only thing she does like a siren, but she does

78

it superbly!"

For a moment it seemed as if Miss Cornelia had succeeded. The doctor smiled; Dale sat down again, her expression altering from one of anxiety to one of amusement. Miss Cornelia opened her lips to dilate further upon Lizzie's eccentricities.

But just then there was a splintering crash of glass from one of the French windows behind her!

Chapter Six:
Detective Anderson Takes Charge

"What's that?"

"Somebody smashed a windowpane!"

"And threw in a stone!"

"Wait a minute, I'll—" The doctor, all alert at once, ran into the alcove and jerked at the terrace door.

"It's bolted at the top, too," called Miss Cornelia. He nodded, without wasting words on a reply, unbolted the door and dashed out into the darkness of the terrace. Miss Cornelia saw him run past the French windows and disappear into blackness. Meanwhile Dale, her listlessness vanished before the shock of the strange occurrence, had gone to the broken window and picked up the stone. It was wrapped in paper; there seemed to be writing on the paper. She closed the terrace door and brought the stone to her aunt.

Miss Cornelia unwrapped the paper and smoothed out the sheet.

Two lines of course, round handwriting sprawled

across it: *Take warning! Leave this house at once! It is threatened with disaster which will involve you if you remain!*

There was no signature.

"Who do you think wrote it?" asked Dale breathlessly.

Miss Cornelia straightened up like a ramrod—indomitable.

"A fool—that's who! If anything was calculated to make me stay here forever, this sort of thing would do it!"

She twitched the sheet of paper angrily.

"But—something may happen, darling!"

"I hope so! That's the reason I—"

She stopped. The doorbell was ringing again—thrilling, insistent. Her niece started at the sound.

"Oh, don't let anybody in!" she besought Miss Cornelia as Billy came in from the hall with his usual air of walking on velvet.

"Key, front door please—bell ring," he explained tersely, taking the key from the table.

Miss Cornelia issued instructions.

"See that the chain is on the door, Billy. Don't open it all the way. And get the visitor's name before you let him in."

She lowered her voice.

"If he says he is Mr. Anderson, let him in and take him to the library."

Billy nodded and disappeared. Dale turned to her aunt, the color out of her cheeks.

"Anderson? Who is Mr. —"

Miss Cornelia did not answer. She thought for a

moment. Then she put her hand on Dale's shoulder in a gesture of protective affection.

"Dale, dear, you know how I love having you here, but it might be better if you went back to the city."

"Tonight, darling?" Dale managed a wan smile. But Miss Cornelia seemed serious.

"There's something *behind* all this disturbance— something I don't understand. But I mean to."

She glanced about to see if the doctor was returning. She lowered her voice. She drew Dale closer to her.

"The man in the library is a detective from police headquarters," she said.

She had expected Dale to show surprise—excitement—but the white mask of horror which the girl turned toward her appalled her. The young body trembled under her hand for a moment like a leaf in the storm.

"Not—the police!" breathed Dale in tones of utter consternation. Miss Cornelia could not understand why the news had stirred her niece so deeply. But there was no time to puzzle it out, she heard crunching steps on the terrace, the doctor was returning.

"Ssh!" she whispered. "It isn't necessary to tell the doctor. I think he's a sort of perambulating bedside gossip and once it's known the police are here we'll *never* catch the criminals!"

When the doctor entered from the terrace, brushing drops of rain from his no longer immaculate evening clothes, Dale was back on her favorite settee and Miss Cornelia was poring over the mysterious missive that had been wrapped about the stone.

"He got away in the shrubbery," said the doctor disgustedly, taking out a handkerchief to fleck the spots of mud from his shoes.

Miss Cornelia gave him the letter of warning. "Read this," she said.

The doctor adjusted a pair of prince-nez — read the two crude sentences over — once — twice. Then he looked shrewdly at Miss Cornelia.

"Were the others like this?" he queried.

She nodded. "Practically."

He hesitated for a moment like a man with an unpleasant social duty to face.

"Miss Van Gorder, may I speak frankly?"

"Generally speaking, I detest frankness," said that lady grimly. "But — go on!"

The doctor tapped the letter. His face was wholly serious.

"I think you *ought* to leave this house," he said bluntly.

"Because of that letter? Humph!" His very seriousness, perversely enough, made her suddenly wish to treat the whole matter as lightly as possible.

The doctor repressed the obvious annoyance of a man who sees a warning, given in all sobriety, unexpectedly taken as a quip.

"There is some deviltry afoot," he persisted. "You are not safe here, Miss Van Gorder."

But if he was persistent in his attitude, so was she in hers.

"I've been safe in all kinds of houses for sixty-odd years," she said lightly. "It's time I had a bit of a change. Besides," she gestured toward her defenses,

83

"this house is as nearly impregnable as I can make it. The window locks are sound enough, the doors are locked, and the keys are there," she pointed to the keys lying on the table. "As for the terrace door you just used," she went on, "I had Billy put an extra bolt on it today. By the way, did you bolt that door again?" She moved toward the alcove.

"Yes, I did," said the doctor quickly, still seeming unconvinced of the wisdom of her attitude.

"Miss Van Gorder, I confess — I'm very anxious for you," he continued. "This letter is — ominous. Have you any enemies?"

"Don't insult me! Of course I have. Enemies are an indication of character."

The doctor's smile held both masculine pity and equally masculine exasperation. He went on more gently.

"Why not accept my hospitality in the village tonight?" he proposed reasonably. "It's a little house but I'll make you comfortable. Or," he threw out his hands in the gesture of one who reasons with a willful child, "if you won't come to me, let me stay here!"

Miss Cornelia hesitated for an instant. The proposition seemed logical enough — more than that — sensible, safe. And yet, some indefinable feeling — hardly strong enough to be called a premonition — kept her from accepting it. Besides, she knew what the doctor did not, that help was waiting across the hall in the library.

"Thank you, no, Doctor," she said briskly, before she had time to change her mind. "I'm not easily frightened. And tomorrow I intend to equip this entire house with burglar alarms on doors and widows!" she went on defiantly. The incident, as far as she was concerned, was closed. She moved on into the alcove.

She tried the terrace door. "There, I knew it!" she said triumphantly. "Doctor—you *didn't* fasten that bolt!"

The doctor seemed a little taken aback. "Oh—I'm sorry—" he said.

"You only pushed it part of the way," she explained. She completed the task and stepped back into the living-room. "The only thing that worries me now is that broken French window," she said thoughtfully. "Anyone can reach a hand through it and open the latch." She came down toward the settee where Dale was sitting. "Please, Doctor!"

"Oh, what are you going to do?" said the doctor, coming out of a brown study.

"I'm going to barricade that window!" said Miss Cornelia firmly, already struggling to lift one end of the settee. But now Dale came to her rescue.

"Oh, darling, you'll hurt yourself. Let me—" and between them, the doctor and Dale moved the heavy settee along until it stood in front of the window in question.

The doctor stood up when the dusty task was finished, wiping his hands.

"It would take a furniture mover to get in there now!" he said airily.

Miss Cornelia smiled.

"Well, Doctor, I'll say good night now—and thank you very much," she said, extending her hand to the doctor, who bowed over it silently. "Don't keep this young lady up too late; she looks tired." She flashed a look at Dale who stood staring out at the night.

"I'll only smoke a cigarette," promised the doctor. Once again his voice had a note of plea in it. "You won't change your mind?" he asked anew.

Miss Van Gorder's smile was obdurate. "I have a great deal of mind," she said. "It takes a long time to change it."

Then, having exercised her feminine privilege of the last word, she sailed out of the room, still smiling, and closed the door behind her.

The doctor seemed a little nettled by her abrupt departure.

"It may be mind," he said, turning back toward Dale, "but forgive me if I say I think it seems more like foolhardy stubbornness!"

Dale turned away from the window. "Then you think there is really danger?"

The doctor's eyes were grave.

"Well, those letters—" he dropped the letter on the table. "They mean *something*. Here you are—isolated—the village two miles away—and enough shrubbery around the place to hide a dozen assassins—"

If his manner had been in the slightest degree melodramatic, Dale would have found the ominous sentences more easy to discount. But this calm, intent statement of fact was a chill touch at her heart. And yet—

"But what enemies can Aunt Cornelia have?" she asked helplessly.

"Any man will tell you what I do," said the doctor with increasing seriousness. He took a cigarette from his case and tapped it on the case to emphasize his words. "This is no place for two women, practically alone."

Dale moved away from him restlessly, to warm her hands at the fire. The doctor gave a quick glance around the room. Then, unseen by her, he stepped noiselessly over to the table, took the matchbox there off its holder and slipped it into his pocket. It seemed a curiously useless and meaningless gesture, but his next words evinced that the action had been deliberate.

"I don't seem to be able to find any matches—" he said with assumed carelessness, fiddling with the matchbox holder.

Dale turned away from the fire. "Oh, aren't there any? I'll get you some," she said with automatic politeness, and departed to search for them.

The doctor watched her go, saw the door close behind her. Instantly his face set into tense and wary lines. He glanced about—then ran lightly into the alcove and noiselessly unfastened the bolt on the terrace door which he had pretended to fasten after his search of the shrubbery. When Dale returned with the matches, he was back where he had been when she had left him, glancing at a magazine on the table.

He thanked her urbanely as she offered him the box.

"So sorry to trouble you—but tobacco is the one drug every doctor forbids his patients and prescribes for himself."

87

Dale smiled at the little joke. He lit his cigarette and drew in the fragrant smoke with apparent gusto. But a moment later he had crushed out the glowing end in an ash tray.

"By the way, has Miss Van Gorder a revolver?" he queried casually, glancing at his wrist watch.

"Yes. She fired it off this afternoon to see if it would work." Dale smiled at the memory.

The doctor, too, seemed amused. "If she tries to shoot anything—for goodness' sake stand behind her!" he advised. He glanced at the wrist watch again. "Well—I must be going—"

"If anything happens," said Dale slowly, "I shall telephone you at once."

Her words seemed to disturb the doctor slightly—but only for a second. He grew even more urbane.

"I'll be home shortly after midnight," he said. "I'm stopping at the Johnsons' on my way. One of their children is ill—or supposed to be." He took a step toward the door, then he turned toward Dale again.

"Take a parting word of advice," he said. "The thing to do with a midnight prowler is—let him alone. Lock your bedroom doors and don't let anything bring you out till morning." He glanced at Dale to see how she took the advice, his hand on the knob of the door.

"Thank you," said Dale seriously. "Good night, Doctor—Billy will let you out, he has the key."

"By Jove!" laughed the doctor, "you *are* careful, aren't you! The place is like a fortress! Well—good night, Miss Dale—"

"Good night." The door closed behind him. Dale

88

was left alone. Suddenly her composure left her, the fixed smile died. She stood gazing ahead at nothing, her face a mask of terror and apprehension. But it was like a curtain that had lifted for a moment on some secret tragedy and then fallen again. When Billy returned with the front door key she was as impassive as he was.

"Has the new gardener come yet?"

"He here," said Billy stolidly. "Name Brook."

She was entirely herself once more when Billy, departing, held the door open wide—to admit Miss Cornelia Van Gorder and a tall, strong-featured man, quietly dressed, with reticent, piercing eyes—the detective!

Dale's first conscious emotion was one of complete surprise. She had expected a heavy-set, blue-jowled vulgarian with a black cigar, a battered derby, and stubby policemen's shoes. *Why this man's a gentleman!* she thought. *At least he looks like one—and yet—you can tell from his face he'd have as little mercy as a steel trap for anyone he had to—catch—* She shuddered uncontrollably.

"Dale, dear," said Miss Cornelia with triumph in her voice. "This is Mr. Anderson."

The newcomer bowed politely, glancing at her casually and then looking away. Miss Cornelia, however, was obviously a fine feather and relishing to the utmost the presence of a real detective in the house.

"This is the room I spoke of," she said briskly. "All the disturbances have taken place around that terrace door."

The detective took three swift steps into the alcove,

89

glanced about it searchingly. He indicated the stairs.

"That is not the main staircase?"

"No, the main staircase is out there." Miss Cornelia waved her hand in the direction of the hall.

The detective came out of the alcove and paused by the French windows.

"I think there must be a conspiracy between the Architects' Association and the Housebreakers' Union these days," he said grimly. "Look at all that glass. All a burglar needs is a piece of putty and a diamond-cutter to break in."

"But the curious thing is," continued Miss Cornelia, "that whoever got into the house evidently had a key to that door." Again she indicated the terrace door, but Anderson did not seem to be listening to her.

"Hello — what's this?" he said sharply, his eye lighting on the broken glass below the shattered French window. He picked up a piece of glass and examined it.

Dale cleared her throat. "It was broken from the outside a few minutes ago," she said.

"The outside?" Instantly the detective had pulled aside a blind and was staring out into the darkness.

"Yes. And then that letter was thrown in." She pointed to the threatening missive on the center table.

Anderson picked it up, glanced through it, laid it down. All his movements were quick and sure — each executed with the minimum expense of effort.

"H'm," he said in a calm voice that held a glint of humor. "Curious, the anonymous letter complex!

Apparently someone considers you an undesirable tenant!"

Miss Cornelia took up the tale.

"There are some things I haven't told you yet," she said. "This house belonged to the late Courtleigh Fleming." He glanced at her sharply.

"The Union Bank?"

"Yes. I rented it for the summer and moved in last Monday. We have not had a really quiet night since I came. The very first night I saw a man with an electric flashlight making his way through the shrubbery!"

"You poor dear!" from Dale sympathetically. "And you were here alone!"

"Well, I had Lizzie. And," said Miss Cornelia with enormous importance, opening the drawer of the center table, "I had my revolver. I know so little about these things, Mr. Anderson, that if I didn't hit a burglar, I knew I'd hit somebody or something!" and she gazed with innocent awe directly down the muzzle of her beloved weapon, then waved it with an airy gesture beneath the detective's nose.

Anderson gave an involuntary start, then his eyes lit up with grim mirth.

"Would you mind putting that away?" he said suavely. "I like to get in the papers as much as anybody, but I don't want to have them say — *omit flowers.*"

Miss Cornelia gave him a glare of offended pride, but he endured it with such quiet equanimity that she merely replaced the revolver in the drawer, with a hurt expression, and waited for him to open the next topic of conversation.

He finished his preliminary survey of the room and returned to her.

"Now you say you don't think anybody has got upstairs yet?" he queried.

Miss Cornelia regarded the alcove stairs.

"I think not. I'm a very light sleeper, especially since the papers have been so full of the exploits of this criminal they call the Bat. He's in them again tonight." She nodded toward the evening paper.

The detective smiled faintly.

"Yes, he's contrived to surround himself with such an air of mystery that it verges on the supernatural — or seems that way to newspapermen."

"I confess," admitted Miss Cornelia, "I've thought of him in this connection." She looked at Anderson to see how he would take the suggestion but the latter merely smiled again, this time more broadly.

"That's going rather a long way for a theory," he said. "And the Bat is not in the habit of giving warnings."

"Nevertheless," she insisted, "somebody has been trying to get into this house, night after night."

The detective smiled ruefully. He picked up the evening paper, glanced at it, shook his head. "I'd forget the Bat in all this. You can always tell when the Bat has had anything to do with a crime. When he's through, he signs his name to it."

Miss Cornelia sat upright. "His name? I thought nobody knew his name?"

The detective made a little gesture of apology. "That was a figure of speech. The newspapers named him the Bat because he moved with incredible rapidity, always at night, and by signing his name I mean he leaves the symbol of his identity—the Bat, which can see in the dark."

"I wish I could," Miss Cornelia, striving to seem unimpressed. "These country lights are always going out."

Anderson's face grew stern. "Sometimes he draws the outline of a bat at the scene of the crime. Once, in some way, he got hold of a real bat, and nailed it to the wall."

Dale, listening, could not repress a shudder at the gruesome picture and Miss Cornelia's hands gave an involuntary twitch as her knitting needles clicked together. Anderson seemed by no means unconscious of the effect he had created.

"How many people in this house, Miss Van Gorder?"

"My niece and myself." Miss Cornelia indicated Dale, who had picked up her wrap and was starting to leave the room. "Lizzie Allen, who has been my personal maid ever since I was a child, the Japanese butler, and the gardener. The cook and the housemaid left this morning—frightened away."

She smiled as she finished her description. Dale reached the door and passed slowly out into the hall. The detective gave her a single, sharp glance as she made her exit. He seemed to think over the factors Miss Cornelia had mentioned.

"Well," he said, after a slight pause, "you can have a good night's sleep tonight. I'll stay right here in the dark and watch."

"Would you like some coffee to keep you awake?"

Anderson nodded. "Thank you." His voice sank lower. "Do the servants know who I am?"

"Only Lizzie, my maid."

His eyes fixed hers. "I wouldn't tell anyone I'm remaining up all night," he said.

A formless fear rose in Miss Cornelia's mind. "You don't suspect my household?" she said in a low voice.

He spoke with emphasis — all the more pronounced because of the quietude of his tone.

"I'm not taking any chances," he said determinedly.

Chapter Seven: Cross-Questions and Crooked Answers

All unconscious of the slur just cast upon her forty years of single-minded devotion to the Van Gorder family, Lizzie chose that particular moment to open the door and make a little bob at her mistress and the detective.

"The gentleman's room is ready," she said meekly. In her mind she was already beseeching her patron saint that she would not have to show the gentleman to his room. Her ideas of detectives were entirely drawn from sensational magazines and her private opinion was that Anderson might have anything in his pocket from a set of terrifying false whiskers to a bomb!

Miss Cornelia, obedient to the detective's instructions, promptly told the whitest of fibs for Lizzie's benefit.

"The maid will show you to your room now and you can make yourself comfortable for the night." There—that would mislead Lizzie, without being quite a lie.

"My toilet is made for an occasion like this when I've got my gun loaded," answered Anderson carelessly. The allusion to the gun made Lizzie start nervously, unhappily for her, for it drew his attention to her and he now transfixed her with a stare.

"This is the maid you referred to?" he inquired. Miss Cornelia assented. He drew nearer to the unhappy Lizzie.

"What's your name?" he asked, turning to her.

"E-Elizabeth Allen," stammered Lizzie, feeling like a small and distrustful sparrow in the toils of an officious python.

Anderson seemed to run through a mental rogues' gallery of other criminals named Elizabeth Allen that he had known.

"How old are you?" he proceeded.

Lizzie looked at her mistress despairingly. "Have I got to answer that?" she wailed. Miss Cornelia nodded inexorably.

Lizzie braced herself. "Thirty-two," she said, with an arch toss of her head.

The detective looked surprised and slightly amused.

"She's fifty if she's a day," said Miss Cornelia treacherously in spite of a look from Lizzie that would have melted a stone.

The trace of a smile appeared and vanished on the detective's face.

"Now, Lizzie," he said sternly, "do you ever walk in your sleep?"

"I do not," said Lizzie indignantly.

"Don't care for the country, I suppose?"

"I do not!"

"Or detectives?" Anderson deigned to be facetious.

"I do not!" There could be no doubt as to the sincerity of Lizzie's answer.

"All right, Lizzie. Be calm. I can stand it," said the detective with treacherous suavity. But he favored her with a long and careful scrutiny before he moved to the table and picked up the note that had been thrown through the window. Quietly he extended it beneath Lizzie's nose.

"Ever see this before?" he said crisply, watching her face.

Lizzie read the note with bulging eyes, her face horror-striken. When she had finished, she made a gesture of wild disclaimer that nearly removed a portion of Anderson's left ear.

"Mercy on us!" she moaned, mentally invoking not only her patron saint but all the rosary of heaven to protect herself and her mistress.

But the detective still kept his eye on her.

"Didn't write it yourself, did you?" he queried curtly.

"I did not!" said Lizzie angrily. "I did *not!*"

"And—you're sure you don't walk in your sleep?"

The bare idea strained Lizzie's nerves to the breaking point.

"When I get into bed in this house I wouldn't put my feet out for a million dollars!" she said with heartfelt candor. Even Anderson was compelled to grin at this.

"Then I won't ask you to," he said, relaxing considerably. "That's more money than I'm worth, Lizzie."

"Well, *I'll say it is!*" quoth Lizzie, now thoroughly

aroused, and flounced out of the room in high dudgeon, her pompadour bristling, before he had time to interrogate her further.

He replaced the note on the table and turned back to Miss Cornelia. If he had found any clue to the mystery in Lizzie's demeanor, she could not read it in his manner.

"Now, what about the butler?" he said.

"Nothing about him — except that he was Courtleigh Fleming's servant."

Anderson paused. "Do you consider that significant?"

A shadow appeared behind him deep in the alcove — a vague, listening figure — Dale, on tiptoe, conspiratorial, taking pains not to draw the attention of the others to her prescence. But both Miss Cornelia and Anderson were too engrossed in their conversation to notice her.

Miss Cornelia hesitated.

"Isn't it possible that there is a connection between the colossal theft at the Union Bank and *these* disturbances?" she said.

Anderson seemed to think over the question.

"What do you mean?" he asked as Dale slowly moved into the room from the alcove, silently closing the alcove doors behind her, and still unobserved.

"Suppose," said Miss Cornelia slowly, "that Courtleigh Fleming took that money from his own bank and concealed it in this house?" The eavesdropper grew rigid.

"That's the theory you gave headquarters, isn't it?" said Anderson. "But I'll tell you how headquarters figures it out. In the first place, the cashier is missing. In the second place, if Courtleigh Fleming did it and got as far as Colorado, he had it with him when he died, and the facts apparently don't bear that out. In the third place, suppose he had hidden the money in or around the house. Why did he rent it to you?"

"But he didn't," said Miss Cornelia obstinately, "I leased this house from his nephew, his heir."

The detective smiled tolerantly.

"Well, I wouldn't struggle like that for a theory," he said, the professional note coming back to his voice. "The cashier's *missing*—that's the answer."

Miss Cornelia resented his offhand demolition of the mental card-castle she had erected with such pride.

"I have read a great deal on the detection of crime," she said hotly, "and—"

"Well, we all have our little hobbies," he said tolerantly. "A good many people rather fancy themselves as detectives and run around looking for clues under the impression that a clue is a big and vital factor that sticks up like—well, like a sore thumb. The fact is that the criminal takes care of the big and important factors. It's only the little ones he may overlook. To go back to your friend the Bat, it's because of his skill in little things that he's still at large."

"Then *you* don't think there's a chance that the money from the Union Bank is in this house?" persisted Miss Cornelia.

"I think it is very unlikely."

Miss Cornelia put her knitting away and rose. She still clung tenaciously to her own theories but her belief in them had been badly shaken.

"If you'll come with me, I'll show you to your room," she said a little stiffly. The detective stepped back to let her pass.

"Sorry to spoil your little theory," he said, and followed her to the door. If either had noticed the unobtrusive listener to their conversation, neither made a sign.

The moment the door had closed on them Dale sprang into action. She seemed a different girl from the one who had left the room so inconspicuously such a short time before. There were two bright spots of color in her cheeks and she was obviously laboring under great excitement. She went quickly to the alcove doors—they opened softly—disclosing the young man who had said that he was Brooks the new gardener—and yet not the same young man—for his assumed air of servitude had dropped from him like a cloak, revealing him as a young fellow at least of the same general social class as Dale's if not a fellow-inhabitant of the select circle where Van Gorders revolved about Van Gorders, and a man's great-grandfather was more important than the man himself.

Dale cautioned him with a warning finger as he advanced into the room.

"Sh! Sh!" she whispered. "Be careful! That man's a detective!"

Brooks gave a hunted glance at the door into the hall.

"Then they've traced me here," he said in a dejected voice.

"I don't think so."

He made a gesture of helplessness.

"I couldn't get back to my rooms," he said in a whisper. "If they've searched them," he paused, "as they're sure to—they'll find your letters to me." He paused again. "Your aunt doesn't suspect anything?"

"No, I told her I'd engaged a gardener—and that's all there was about it."

He came nearer to her. "Dale!" he murmured in a tense voice. "You *know* I didn't take that money!" he said with boyish simplicity.

All the loyalty of first-love was in her answer.

"Of course! I believe in you absolutely!" she said. He caught her in his arms and kissed her—gratefully, passionately. Then the galling memory of the predicament in which he stood, the hunt already on his trail, came back to him. He released her gently, still holding one of her hands.

"But—the police here!" he stammered, turning away. "What does that mean?"

Dale swiftly informed him of the situation.

"Aunt Cornelia says people have been trying to break into the house for days—at night."

Brooks ran his hand through his hair in a gesture of bewilderment. Then he seemed to catch at a hope.

"What sort of people?" he queried sharply.

Dale was puzzled. "She doesn't know."

The excitement in her lover's manner came to a head. "That proves exactly what I've contended right along," he said, thudding one fist softly in the palm of the other. "Through some underneath channel old Fleming had been selling those securities for months,

101

turning them into cash. And somebody knows about it, and knows that that money is hidden here. Don't you see? Your Aunt Cornelia has crabbed the game by coming here."

"Why didn't you tell the police that? Now they think, because you ran away—"

"Ran away! The only chance I had was a few hours to myself to try to prove what actually happened."

"Why don't you tell the detective what you think?" said Dale at her wits' end. "That Courtleigh Fleming took the money and that it is still here?"

Her lover's face grew somber.

"He'd take me into custody at once and I'd have no chance to search."

He was searching now. His eyes roved about the living-room—walls—ceiling—hopefully—desperately—looking for a clue—the tiniest clue to support his theory.

"Why are you so sure it is here?" queried Dale.

Brooks explained. "You must remember Fleming was no ordinary defaulter and *he* had no intention of being exiled to a foreign country. He wanted to come back here and take his place in the community while I was in the pen."

"But even then—"

He interrupted her. "Listen, dear—" He crossed to the billiard-room door, closed it firmly, returned.

"The architect that built this house was an old friend of mine," he said in hushed accents. "We were together in France and you know the way fellows get to talking when they're far away and cut off—" He paused, seeing the cruel gleam of the flame throwers—two figures huddled in a foxhole, whiling away the terrible hours of waiting by muttered talk.

"Just an hour or two before—a shell got this friend of mine," he resumed, "he told me he had built a hidden room in this house."

"Where?" gasped Dale.

Brooks shook his head. "I don't know. We never got to finish that conversation. But I remember what he said. He said, 'You watch old Fleming. If I get mine over here it won't break his heart. He didn't want any living being to know about that room.'"

Now Dale was as excited as he.

"Then you think the money is in this hidden room?"

"I do," said Brooks decidedly. "I don't think Fleming took it away with him. He was too shrewd for that. No, he meant to come back all right, the minute he got the word the bank had been looted. And he'd fixed things so I'd be railroaded to prison—you wouldn't understand, but it was pretty neat. And then the fool nephew rents this house the minute he's dead, and whoever knows about the money—"

"Jack! Why isn't it the nephew who is trying to break in?"

"He wouldn't *have* to break in. He could make an excuse and come in any time."

He clenched his hands despairingly.

"If I could only get hold of a blueprint of this place!" he muttered.

Dale's face fell. It was sickening to be so close to the secret—and yet not find it. "Oh, Jack, I'm so confused and worried!" she confessed, with a little sob.

Brooks put his hands on her shoulders in an effort to cheer her spirits.

"Now listen, dear," he said firmly, "this isn't as hard as it sounds. I've got a clear night to work in—and as true as I'm standing here, that money's in this house. Listen, honey—it's like this." He pantomimed the old nursery rhyme of *The House that Jack Built*. "Here's the house that Courtleigh Fleming built—here, somewhere, is the Hidden Room in the house that Courtleigh Fleming built—and here—somewhere—pray heaven—is the money—in the Hidden Room—in the house that Courtleigh Fleming built. When you're low in your mind, just say that over!"

She managed a faint smile. "I've forgotten it already," she said, drooping.

He still strove for an offhand gaiety that he did not feel.

"Why, look here!" and she followed the play of his hands obediently, like a tired child "it's a sort of game, dearest. 'Money, money—who's got the money?' *You* know!" For the dozenth time he stared at the unrevealing walls of the room. "For that matter," he added, "the Hidden Room may be behind these very walls."

He looked about for a tool, a poker, anything that would sound the walls and test them for hollow spaces. Ah, he had it—that driver in the bag of golf clubs over in the corner. He got the driver and stood wondering where he had best begin. That blank wall above the fireplace looked as promising as any. He tapped it gently with the golf club—afraid to make

104

too much noise and yet anxious to test the wall as thoroughly as possible. A dull, heavy reverberation answered his stroke—nothing hollow there apparently.

As he tried another spot, again thunder beat the long roll on its iron drum outside, in the night. The lights blinked—wavered—recovered.

"The lights are going out again," said Dale dully, her excitement sunk into a stupefied calm.

"Let them go! The less light the better for me. The only thing to do is to go over this house room by room." He pointed to the billiard-room door. "What's in there?"

"The billiard room." She was thinking hard. "Jack! Perhaps Courtleigh Fleming's nephew would know where the blueprints are!"

He looked dubious. "It's a chance, but not a very good one," he said. "Well—" He led the way into the billiard room and began to rap at random upon its walls while Dale listened intently for any echo that might betray the presence of a hidden chamber of sliding panel.

Thus it happened that Lizzie received the first real thrill of what was to prove to her—and to others—a sensational and hideous night. For, coming into the living-room to lay a cloth for Mr. Anderson's night supper, not only did the lights blink threateningly and the thunder roll, but a series of spirit raps was certainly to be heard coming from the region of the billiard room.

"Oh, my God!" she wailed, and the next instant the lights went out, leaving her in inky darkness.

With a loud shriek she bolted out of the room.

Thunder—lightning—dashing of rain on the streaming glass of the windows—the storm hallooing its hounds. Dale huddled close to her lover as they groped their way back to the living-room, cautiously, doing their best to keep from stumbling against some heavy piece of furniture whose fall would arouse the house.

"There's a candle on the table, Jack, if I can find the table." Her outstretched hands touched a familiar object. "Here it is." She fumbled for a moment. "Have you any matches?"

"Yes." He struck one—another—lit the candle—set it down on the table. In the weak glow of the little taper, whose tiny flame illuminated but a portion of the living-room, his face looked tense and strained.

"It's pretty nearly hopeless," he said, "if all the walls are paneled like that."

As if in mockery of his words and his quest, a muffled knocking that seemed to come from the ceiling of the very room he stood in answered his despair.

"What's that?" gasped Dale.

They listened. The knocking was repeated—knock—knock—knock—knock.

"Someone else is looking for the Hidden Room!" muttered Brooks, gazing up at the ceiling intently, as if he could tear from it the secret of this new mystery by sheer strength of will.

Chapter Eight:
The Gleaming Eye

"It's upstairs!" Dale took a step toward the alcove stairs. Brooks halted her.

"Who's in this house besides ourselves?" he queried.

"Only the detective, Aunt Cornelia, Lizzie, and Billy."

"Billy's the Jap?"

"Yes."

Brooks paused an instant. "Does he belong to your aunt?"

"No. He was Courtleigh Fleming's butler."

Knock — knock — knock — knock — the dull, methodical rapping on the ceiling of the living-room began again.

"Courtleigh Fleming's butler, eh?" muttered Brooks. He put down his candle and stole noiselessly into the alcove. "It may be the Jap!" he whispered.

Knock — knock — knock — knock! This time the mysterious rapping seemed to come from the upper hall.

"If it is the Jap, I'll get him!" Brooks's voice was tense with resolution. He hesitated—made for the hall door—tiptoed out into the darkness around the main staircase, leaving Dale alone in the living-room beset by shadowy terrors.

Utter silence succeeded his noiseless departure. Even the storm lulled for a moment. Dale stood thinking, wondering, searching desperately for some way to help her lover.

At last a resolution formed in her mind. She went to the city telephone.

"Hello," she said in a low voice, glancing over her shoulder now and then to make sure she was not overheard. "1—2—4—please—yes, that's right. Hello—is that the country club? Is Mr. Richard Fleming there? Yes, I'll hold the wire."

She looked about nervously. Had something moved in that corner of blackness where her candle did not pierce? No! How silly of her!

Buzz-buzz on the telephone. She picked up the receiver again.

"Hello—is this Mr. Fleming? This is Miss Ogden— Dale Ogden. I know it must seem odd my calling you this late, but—I wonder if you could come over here for a few minutes. Yes—tonight." Her voice grew stronger. "I wouldn't trouble you but—it's awfully important. Hold the wire a moment." She put down the phone and made another swift survey of the room, listened furtively at the door—all clear! She returned to the phone.

"Hello—Mr. Fleming—I'll wait outside the house on the drive. It—it's a confidential matter. Thank you so much."

She hung up the phone, relieved—not an instant too soon, for, as she crossed toward the fireplace to add a new log to the dying glow of the fire, the hall door opened and Anderson, the detective, came softly in with an unlighted candle in his hand.

Her composure almost deserted her. How much had he heard? What deduction would he draw if he had heard? An assignation, perhaps! Well, she could stand that; she could stand anything to secure the next few hours of liberty for Jack. For that length of time she and the law were at war; she and this man were at war.

But his first words relieved her fears.

"Spooky sort of place in the dark, isn't it?" he said casually.

"Yes, rather." If he would only go away before Brooks came back or Richard Fleming arrived! But he seemed in a distressingly chatty frame of mind.

"Left me upstairs without a match," continued Anderson. "I found my way down by walking part of the way and falling the rest. Don't suppose I'll ever find the room I left my toothbrush in!" He laughed, lighting the candle in his hand from the candle on the table.

"You're not going to stay up all night, are you?" said Dale nervously, hoping he would take the hint. But he seemed entirely oblivious of such minor considerations as sleep. He took out a cigar.

"Oh, I may doze a bit," he said. He eyed her with a certain approval. She was a darned pretty girl and she looked intelligent. "I suppose you have a theory of your own about these intrusions you've been having here? Or apparently having."

"I knew nothing about them until tonight."

"Still," he persisted conversationally, "you know about them now." But when she remained silent, "Is Miss Van Gorder usually — of a nervous temperament? Imagines she sees things, and all that?"

"I don't think so." Dale's voice was strained. Where was Brooks? What had happened to him?

Anderson puffed on his cigar, pondering. "Know the Flemings?" he asked.

"I've met Mr. Richard Fleming once or twice."

Something in her tone caused him to glance at her. "Nice fellow?"

"I don't know him at all well."

"Know the cashier of the Union Bank?" he shot at her suddenly.

"No!" She strove desperately to make the denial convincing but she could not hide the little tremor in her voice.

The detective mused.

"Fellow of good family, I understand," he said, eyeing her. "Very popular. That's what's behind most of these bank embezzlements; men getting into society and spending more than they make."

Dale hailed the tinkle of the city telephone with an inward sigh of relief. The detective moved to answer the house phone on the wall by the alcove, mistaking the direction of the ring.

Dale corrected him quickly.

"No, the other one. That's the house phone."

Anderson looked the apparatus over.

"No connection with the outside, eh?"

"No," Dale said absent-mindedly. "Just from room to room in the house."

He accepted her explanation and answered the other telephone.

"Hello — hello — what the —" He moved the receiver hook up and down, without result, and gave it up. "This line sounds dead," he said.

"It was all right a few minutes ago," said Dale without thinking.

"You were using it a few minutes ago?"

She hesitated — what use to deny what she had already admitted, for all practical purposes.

"Yes."

The city telephone rang again. The detective pounced upon it.

"Hello — yes — yes — this is Anderson — go ahead." He paused, while the tiny voice in the receiver buzzed for some seconds. Then he interrupted it impatiently.

"You're sure of that, are you? I see. All right. 'By."

He hung up the receiver and turned swiftly on Dale.

"Did I understand you to say that you were not acquainted with the cashier of the Union Bank?" he said to her with a new note in his voice.

Dale stared ahead of her blankly. It had come! She did not reply.

Anderson went on ruthlessly.

"That was headquarters, Miss Ogden. They have found some letters in Bailey's room which seem to indicate that you were not telling the entire truth just now."

111

He paused, waiting for her answer. "What letters?" she said wearily.

"From you to Jack Bailey—showing that you had recently become engaged to him."

Dale decided to make a clean breast of it, or as clean a one as she dared.

"Very well," she said in an even voice, "that's true."

"Why didn't you say so before?" There was menace beneath his suavity.

She thought swiftly. Apparent frankness seemed to be the only resource left her. She gave him a candid smile.

"It's been a secret. I haven't even told my aunt yet." Now she let indignation color her tones. "How can the police be so stupid as to accuse Jack Bailey, a young man and about to be married? Do you think he would wreck his future like that?"

"Some people wouldn't call it wrecking a future to lay away a million dollars," said Anderson ominously. He came closer to Dale, fixing her with his eyes. "Do you know *where* Bailey is now?" He spoke slowly and menacingly.

She did not flinch.

"No."

The detective paused.

"Miss Ogden," he said, still with that hidden threat in his voice, "in the last minute or so the Union Bank case and certain things in this house have begun to tie up pretty close together. Bailey disappeared this morning. Have you heard from him since?"

Her eyes met his without weakening, her voice was cool and composed.

112

"No."

The detective did not comment on her answer. She could not tell from his face whether he thought she had told the truth or lied. He turned away from her brusquely.

"I'll ask you to bring Miss Van Gorder here," he said in his professional voice.

"Why do you want her?" Dale blazed at him rebelliously.

He was quiet. "Because this case it taking on a new phase."

"You don't think I know anything about that money?" she said, a little wildly, hoping that a display of sham anger might throw him off the trail he seemed to be following.

He seemed to accept her words, cynically, at their face value.

"No," he said, "but you know somebody who does."

Dale hesitated, sought for a biting retort, found none. It did not matter; any respite, no matter how momentary, from these probing questions, would be a relief. She silently took one of the lighted candles and left the living-room to search for her aunt.

Left alone, the detective reflected for a moment, then picking up the one lighted candle that remained, commenced a systematic examination of the living-room. His methods were thorough, but it, when he came to the end of his quest, he had made any new discoveries, the reticent composure of his face did not betray the fact. When he had finished he turned patiently toward the billiard room — the little flame of

113

his candle was swallowed up in its dark recesses—he closed the door of the living-room behind him. The storm was dying away now, but a few flashes of lightning still flickered, lighting up the darkness of the deserted living-room now and then with a harsh, brief glare.

A lightning flash—a shadow cast abruptly on the shade of one of the French windows, to disappear as abruptly as the flash was blotted out—the shadow of a man—a prowler—feeling his way through the lightning-slashed darkness to the terrace door. The detective? Brooks? The Bat? The lightning flash was too brief for any observer to have recognized the stealing shape—if any observer had been there.

But the lack of an observer was promptly remedied. Just as the shadowy shape reached the terrace door and its shadow-fingers closed over the knob, Lizzie entered the deserted living-room on stumbling feet. She was carrying a tray of dishes and food—some cold meat on a platter, a cup and saucer, a roll, a butter pat—and she walked slowly, with terror only one leap behind her and blank darkness ahead.

She had only reached the table and was preparing to deposit her tray and beat a shameful retreat, when a sound behind her made her turn. The key in the door from the terrace to the alcove had clicked. Paralyzed with fright she stared and waited, and the next moment a formless thing, a blacker shadow in a world of shadows, passed swiftly in and up the small staircase.

But not only a shadow. To Lizzie's terrified eyes it bore an eye, a single gleaming eye, just above the level of the stair rail, and this eye was turned on her.

It was too much. She dropped the tray on the table with a crash and gave vent to a piercing shriek that would have shamed the siren of a fire engine.

Miss Cornelia and Anderson, rushing in from the hall and the billiard room respectively, each with a lighted candle, found her gasping and clutching at the table for support.

"For the love of heaven, what's wrong?" cried Miss Cornelia irritatedly. The coffeepot she was carrying in her other hand spilled a portion of its boiling contents on Lizzie's shoe and Lizzie screamed anew and began to dance up and down on the uninjured foot.

"Oh, my foot—my foot!" she squealed hysterically. "My foot!"

Miss Cornelia tried to shake her back to her senses.

"My patience! Did you yell like that because you stubbed your toe?"

"You scalded it!" cried Lizzie wildly. "It went up the staircase!"

"Your *toe* went up the staircase?"

"No, no! An eye—an eye as big as a saucer! It ran right up that staircase—" She indicated the alcove with a trembling forefinger. Miss Cornelia put her coffeepot and her candle down on the table and opened her mouth to express her frank opinion of her factotum's sanity. But here the detective took charge.

"Now see here," he said with some sternness to the quaking Lizzie, "stop this racket and tell me what you saw!"

115

"A ghost!" persisted Lizzie, still hopping around on one leg. "It came right through that door and ran up the stairs—oh—" and she seemed prepared to scream again as Dale, white-faced, came in from the hall, followed by Billy and Brooks, the latter holding still another candle.

"Who screamed?" said Dale tensely.

"I did!" Lizzie wailed, "I saw a ghost!" She turned to Miss Cornelia. "I begged you not to come here," she vociferated. "I begged you on my bended knees. There's a graveyard not a quarter of a mile away."

"Yes, and one more scare like that, Lizzie Allen, and you'll have me lying in it," said her mistress unsympathetically. She moved up to examine the scene of Lizzie's ghostly misadventure, while Anderson began to interrogate its heroine.

"Now, Lizzie," he said, forcing himself to urbanity, "what did you really see?"

"I told you what I saw."

His manner grew somewhat threatening.

"You're not trying to frighten Miss Van Gorder into leaving this house and going back to the city?"

"Well, if I am," said Lizzie with grim, unconscious humor, "I'm giving myself an awful good scare, too, ain't I?"

The two glared at each other as Miss Cornelia returned from her survey of the alcove.

"Somebody who had a key could have got in here, Mr. Anderson," she said annoyedly. "That terrace door's been unbolted from the inside."

Lizzie groaned. "I told you so," she wailed. "I knew something was going to happen tonight. I

116

heard rappings all over the house today, and the ouija-board spelled Bat!"

The detective recovered his poise. "I think I see the answer to your puzzle, Miss Van Gorder," he said, with a scornful glance at Lizzie. "A hysterical and not very reliable woman, anxious to go back to the city and terrified over and over by the shutting off of the electric lights."

If looks could slay, his characterization of Lizzie would have laid him dead at her feet at that instant. Miss Van Gorder considered his theory.

"I wonder," she said.

The detective rubbed his hands together more cheerfully.

"A good night's sleep and—" he began, but the irrepressible Lizzie interrupted him.

"My God, we're not going to bed, are we?" she said, with her eyes as big as saucers.

He gave her a kindly pat on the shoulder, which she obviously resented.

"You'll feel better in the morning," he said. "Lock your door and say your prayers, and leave the rest to me."

Lizzie muttered something inaudible and rebellious, but now Miss Cornelia added her protestations to his.

"That's very good advice," she said decisively. "You take her, Dale."

Reluctantly, with a dragging of feet and scared glances cast back over her shoulder, Lizzie allowed herself to be drawn toward the door and the main staircase by Dale. But she did not depart without one

117

Parthian shot.

"I'm not going to bed!" she wailed as Dale's strong young arm helped her out into the hall. "Do you think I want to wake up in the morning with my throat cut?" Then the creaking of the stairs, and Dale's soothing voice reassuring her as she painfully clambered toward the third floor, announced that Lizzie, for some time at least, had been removed as an active factor from the puzzling equation of Cedarcrest.

Anderson confronted Miss Cornelia with certain relief.

"There are certain things I want to discuss with you, Miss Van Gorder," he said. "But they can wait until tomorrow morning."

Miss Cornelia glanced about the room. His manner was reassuring.

"Do you think all this—pure imagination?" she said.

"Don't you?"

She hesitated, "I'm not sure."

He laughed. "I'll tell you what I'll do. You go upstairs and go to bed comfortably. I'll make a careful search of the house before I settle down, and if I find anything at all suspicious, I'll promise to let you know."

She agreed to that, and after sending the Jap out for more coffee prepared to go upstairs.

Never had the thought of her own comfortable bed appealed to her so much. But, in spite of her weariness, she could not quite resign herself to take Lizzie's story as lightly as the detective seemed to.

118

"If what Lizzie says is true," she said, taking her candle, "the upper floors of the house are even less safe than this one."

"I imagine Lizzie's account just now is about as reliable as her previous one as to her age," Anderson assured her. "I'm certain you need not worry. Just go on up and get your beauty sleep; I'm sure you need it."

On which ambiguous remark Miss Van Gorder took her leave, rather grimly smiling.

It was after she had gone that Anderson's glance fell on Brooks, standing warily in the doorway.

"What are you? The gardener?"

But Brooks was prepared for him.

"Ordinarily I drive a car," he said. "Just now I'm working on the place here."

Anderson was observing him closely, with the eyes of a man ransacking his memory for a name—a picture. "I've seen you somewhere—" he went on slowly. "And I'll—place you before long." There was a little threat in his shrewd scrutiny. He took a step toward Brooks.

"Not in the portrait gallery at headquarters, are you?"

"Not yet." Brooks's voice was resentful. Then he remembered his pose and his back grew supple, his whole attitude that of the respectful servant.

"Well, we slip up now and then," said the detective slowly. Then, apparently, he gave up his search for the name—the pictured face. But his manner was still suspicious.

"All right, Brooks," he said tersely. "if you're

119

needed in the night, you'll be *called!*"

Brooks bowed, "Very well, sir." He closed the door softly behind him, glad to have escaped as well as he had.

But that he had not entirely lulled the detective's watchfullness to rest was evident as soon as he had gone. Anderson waited a few seconds, then moved noiselessly over to the hall door—listened—opened it suddenly—closed it again. Then he proceeded to examine the alcove—the stairs, where the gleaming eye had wavered like a corpse-candle before Lizzie's affrighted vision. He tested the terrace door and bolted it. How much truth had there been in her story? He could not decide, but he drew out his revolver nevertheless and gave it a quick inspection to see if it was in working order. A smile crept over his face—the smile of a man who has dangerous work to do and does not shrink from the prospect. He put the revolver back in his pocket and, taking the one lighted candle remaining, went out by the hall door.

For a moment, in the living-room, except for the thunder, all was silence. Then the creak of surreptitious footsteps broke the stillness—light footsteps descending the alcove stairs where the gleaming eye had passed.

It was Dale slipping out of the house to keep her appointment with Richard Fleming. She carried a raincoat over her arm and a pair of rubbers in one hand. Her other hand held a candle. By the terrace door she paused, unbolted it, glanced out into the streaming night with a shiver. Then she came into the living-room and sat down to put on her rubbers.

Hardly had she begun to do so when she started up again. A muffled knocking sounded at the terrace door. It was ominous and determined, and in a panic of terror she rose to her feet. If it was the law, come after Jack, what should she do? Or again, suppose it was the Unknown who had threatened them with death? Not coherent thoughts these, but chaotic, bringing panic with them. Almost unconscious of what she was doing, she reached into the drawer beside her, secured the revolver there and leveled it at the door.

Chapter Nine: A Shot in the Dark

A key clicked in the terrace door—a voice swore muffledly at the rain. Dale lowered her revolver slowly. It was Richard Fleming—come to meet her here, instead of down by the drive.

She had telephoned him on an impulse. But now, as she looked at him in the light of her single candle, she wondered if this rather dissipated, rather foppish young man about town, in his early thirties, could possibly understand and appreciate the motives that had driven her to seek his aid. Still, it was for Jack! She clenched her teeth and resolved to go through with the plan mapped out in her mind. It might be a desperate expedient but she had nowhere else to turn!

Fleming shut the terrace door behind him and moved down from the alcove, trying to shake the rain from his coat.

"Did I frighten you?"

"Oh, Mr. Fleming—yes!" Dale laid her aunt's revolver down on the table. Fleming perceived her nervousness and made a gesture of apology.

"I'm sorry," he said, "I rapped but nobody seemed to hear me, so I used my key."

"You're wet through—I'm sorry," said Dale with mechanical politeness.

He smiled. "Oh, no." He stripped off his cap and raincoat and placed them on a chair, brushing himself off as he did so with finicky little movements of his hands.

"Reggie Beresford brought me over in his car," he said. "He's waiting down the drive."

Dale decided not to waste words in the usual commonplaces of social greeting.

"Mr. Fleming, I'm in dreadful trouble!" she said, facing him squarely, with a courageous appeal in her eyes.

He made a polite movement. "Oh, I say! That's too bad."

She plunged on. "You know the Union Bank closed today."

He laughed lightly.

"Yes, I know it! I didn't have anything in it—or any other bank for that matter," he admitted ruefully, "but I hate to see the old thing go to smash."

Dale wondered which angle was best from which to present her appeal.

"Well, even if you haven't lost anything in this bank failure, a lot of your friends have—surely?" she went on.

"I'll say so!" said Fleming, debonairly. "Beresford is sitting down the road in his Packard now writhing with pain!"

Dale hesitated; Fleming's lightness seemed so incorrigible that, for a moment, she was on the verge of giving her project up entirely. Then, *Waster or*

123

not—he's the only man who can help us! she told herself and continued.

"Lots of awfully poor people are going to suffer, too," she said wistfully.

Fleming chuckled, dismissing the poor with a wave of his hand.

"Oh, well, the poor are always in trouble," he said with airy heartlessness. "They specialize in suffering."

He extracted a monogrammed cigarette from a thin gold case.

"But look here," he went on, moving closer to Dale, "you didn't send for me to discuss this hypothetical poor depositor, did you? Mind if I smoke?"

"No." He lit his cigarette and puffed at it with enjoyment while Dale paused, summoning up her courage. Finally the words came in a rush.

"Mr. Fleming, I'm going to say something rather brutal. Please don't mind. I'm merely—desperate! You see, I happen to be engaged to the cashier, Jack Bailey—"

Fleming whistled. "I *see!* And he's beat it!"

Dale blazed with indignation.

"He has not! I'm going to tell you something. He's here, now, in this house—" she continued fierily, all her defenses thrown aside. "My aunt thinks he's a new gardener. He is here, Mr. Fleming, because he knows he didn't take the money, and the only person who could have done it was—your uncle!"

Dick Fleming dropped his cigarette in a convenient ash tray and crushed it out there, absently, not seeming to notice whether it scorched his fingers or no.

He rose and took a turn about the room. Then he came back to Dale.

"That's a pretty strong indictment to bring against a dead man," he said slowly, seriously.

"It's true!" Dale insisted stubbornly, giving him glance for glance.

Fleming nodded. "All right."

He smiled—a smile that Dale didn't like.

"Suppose it's true—where do I come in?" he said. "You don't think I know where the money is?"

"No," admitted Dale, "but I think you might help to find it."

She went swiftly over to the hall door and listened tensely for an instant. Then she came back to Fleming.

"If anybody comes in—you've just come to get something of yours," she said in a low voice. He nodded understandingly. She dropped her voice still lower.

"Do you know anything about a Hidden Room in this house?" she asked.

Dick Fleming stared at her for a moment. Then he burst into laughter.

"A Hidden Room—that's rich!" he said, still laughing. "Never heard of it! Now, let me get this straight. The idea is—a Hidden Room—and the money is in it—is that it?"

Dale nodded a "Yes."

"The architect who built this house told Jack Bailey that he had built a Hidden Room in it," she persisted.

For a moment Dick Fleming stared at her as if he

could not believe his ears. Then, slowly, his expression changed. Beneath the well-fed, debonair mask of the clubman about town, other lines appeared — lines of avarice and calculation — wolf-marks, betokening the craft and petty ruthlessness of the small soul within the gentlemanly shell. His eyes took on a shifty, uncertain stare — they no longer looked at Dale — their gaze seemed turned inward, beholding a visioned treasure, a glittering pile of gold. And yet, the change in his look was not so pronounced as to give Dale pause — she felt a vague uneasiness steal over her, true — but it would have taken a shrewd and long-experienced woman of the world to read the secret behind Fleming's eyes at first glance — and Dale, for all her courage and common sense, was a young and headstrong girl.

She watched him, puzzled, wondering why he made no comment on her last statement.

"Do you know where there are any blueprints of the house?" she asked at last.

An odd light glittered in Fleming's eyes for a moment. Then it vanished — he held himself in check — the casual idler again.

"Blueprints?" He seemed to think it over. "Why — there may be some. Have you looked in the old secretary in the library? My uncle used to keep all sorts of papers there," he said with apparent helpfulness.

"Why, don't you remember — you locked it when we took the house."

"So I did." Fleming took out his key ring, selected a key. "Suppose you go and look," he said. "Don't you think I better stay here?"

"Oh, *yes* — " said Dale, blinded to everything else by the rising hope in her heart. "Oh, I can hardly thank you enough!" and before he could even reply, she had taken the key and was hurrying toward the hall door.

He watched her leave the room, a bleak smile on his face. As soon as she had closed the door behind her, his languor dropped from him. He became a hound — a ferret — questing for its prey. He ran lightly over to the bookcase by the hall door — a moment's inspection — he shook his head. Perhaps the other bookcase near the French windows — no — it wasn't there. Ah, the bookcase over the fireplace! He remembered now! He made for it, hastily swept the books from the top shelf, reached groping fingers into the space behind the second row of books. There! A dusty roll of three blueprints! He unrolled them hurriedly and tried to make out the white tracings by the light of the fire — no — better take them over to the candle on the table.

He peered at them hungrily in the little spot of light thrown by the candle. The first one — no — nor the second — but the third — the bottom one — good heavens! He took in the significance of the blurred white lines with greedy eyes, his lips opening in a silent exclamation of triumph. Then he pondered for an instant, the blueprint itself was an awkward size — bulky — good, he had it! He carefully tore a small portion from the third blueprint and was about to stuff it in the inside pocket of his dinner jacket when Dale, returning, caught him before he had time to conceal his find. She took in the situation at once.

"Oh, you found it!" she said in tones of rejoicing, giving him back the key to the secretary. Then, as he still made no move to transfer the scrap of blue paper to her, "Please let me have it, Mr. Fleming. I *know* that's it."

Dick Fleming's lips set in a thin line. "Just a moment," he said, putting the table between them with a swift movement. Once more he stole a glance at the scrap of paper in his hand by the flickering light of the candle. Then he faced Dale boldly.

"Do you suppose, if that money is actually here, that I can simply turn this over to you and let you give it to Bailey?" he said. "Every man has his price. How do I know that Bailey's isn't a million dollars?"

Dale felt as if he had dashed cold water in her face.

"What do you mean to do with it then?" she said.

Fleming turned the blueprint over in his hand.

"I don't know," he said. "What is it you want me to do?"

But by now Dale's vague distrust in him had grown very definite.

"Aren't you going to give it to me?"

He put her off. "I'll have to think about that." He looked at the blueprint again. "So the missing cashier is in this house posing as a gardener?" he said with a sneer in his tones.

Dale's temper was rising.

"If you won't give it to me — there's a detective in this house," she said, with a stamp of her foot. She made a movement as if to call Anderson — then, remembering Jack, turned back to Fleming.

"Give it to the detective and let him search," she

pleaded.

"A detective?" said Fleming startled. "What's a detective doing here?"

"People have been trying to break in."

"What people?"

"I don't know."

Fleming stared out beyond Dale, into the night.

"Then it *is* here," he muttered to himself.

Behind his back—was it a gust of air that moved them?—the double doors of the alcove swung open just a crack. Was a listener crouched behind those doors—or was it only a trick of carpentry—a gesture of chance?

The mask of the clubman dropped from Fleming completely. His lips drew back from his teeth in the snarl of a predatory animal that clings to its prey at the cost of life or death.

Before Dale could stop him, he picked up the discarded blueprints and threw them on the fire, retaining only the precious scrap in his hand. The roll blackened and burst into flame. He watched it, smiling.

"I'm not going to give this to any detective," he said quietly, tapping the piece of paper in his hand.

Dale's heart pounded sickeningly but she kept her courage up.

"What do you mean?" she said fiercely. "What are you going to do?"

He faced her across the fireplace, his airy manner coming back to him just enough to add an additional touch of the sinister to the cold self-revelation of his words.

"Let us suppose a few things, Miss Ogden." he said. "Suppose *my* price is a million dollars. Suppose I need money very badly and my uncle has left me a house containing that amount in cash. Suppose I choose to consider that that money is mine—then it wouldn't be hard to suppose, would it, that I'd make a pretty sincere attempt to get away with it?"

Dale summoned all of her fortitude.

"If you go out of this room with that paper I'll scream for help!" she said defiantly.

Fleming made a little mock-bow of courtesy. He smiled.

"To carry on our little game of supposing," he said easily, "suppose there is a detective in this house—and that, if I were concerned, I should tell him where to lay his hands on *Jack Bailey.* Do you suppose you would scream?"

Dale's hands dropped, powerless, at her sides. If only she hadn't told him—too late!—she was helpless. She could not call the detective without ruining Jack—and yet, if Fleming escaped with the money—how could Jack ever prove his innocence?

Fleming watched her for an instant, smiling. Then, seeing she made no move, he darted hastily toward the double doors of the alcove, flung them open, seemed about to dash up the alcove stairs. The sight of him escaping with the only existing clue to the hidden room galvanized Dale into action. She followed him, hurriedly snatching up Miss Cornelia's revolver from the table as she did so, in a last gesture of desperation.

"No! No! Give it to me! Give it to me!" and she

sprang after him, clutching the revolver. He waited for her on the bottom step of the stairs, the slight smile on his face.

Panting breaths in the darkness of the alcove—a short, furious scuffle—he had wrested the revolver away from her, but in doing so had unguarded the precious blueprint. She snatched at it desperately, tearing most of it away, leaving only a corner in his hand. He swore—tried to get it back; she jerked away.

Then suddenly a bright shaft of light split the darkness of the alcove stairs like a sword, a spot of brilliance centered on Fleming's face like the glare of a flashlight focused from above by an invisible hand. For an instant it revealed him, his features distorted with fury, about to rush down the stairs again and attack the trembling girl at their foot.

A single shot rang out. For a second, the fury on Fleming's face seemed to change to a strange look of bewilderment and surprise.

Then the shaft of light was extinguished as suddenly as the snuffing of a candle, and he crumpled forward to the foot of the stairs—struck—lay on his face in the darkness, just inside the double doors.

Dale gave a little whimpering cry of horror.

"Oh, no, no, no," she whispered from a dry throat, automatically stuffing her portion of the precious scrap of blueprint into the bosom of her dress. She stood frozen, not daring to move, not daring even to reach down with her hand and touch the body of Fleming to see if he was dead or alive.

A murmur of excited voices sounded from the hall.

The door flew open, feet stumbled through the darkness—"The noise came from this room!" that was Anderson's voice—"Holy Virgin!" that must be Lizzie—

Even as Dale turned to face the assembled household, the house lights, extinguished since the storm, came on in full brilliance—revealing her to them, standing beside Fleming's body with Miss Cornelia's revolver between them.

She shuddered, seeing Fleming's arm flung out awkwardly by his side. No living man could lie in such a posture.

"I didn't do it! I didn't do it!" she stammered, after a tense silence that followed the sudden reillumining of the lights. Her eyes wandered from figure to figure idly, noting unimportant details. Billy was still in his white coat and his face, impassive as ever, showed not the slightest surprise. Brooks and Anderson were likewise completely dressed, but Miss Cornelia had evidently begun to retire for the night when she had heard the shot—her transformation was askew and she wore a dressing-gown. As for Lizzie, that worthy shivered in a gaudy wrapper adorned with incredible orange flowers, with her hair done up in curlers. Dale saw it all and was never after to forget one single detail of it.

The detective was beside her now, examining Fleming's body with professional thoroughness. At last he rose.

"He's dead," he said quietly. A shiver ran through the watching group. Dale felt a stifling hand constrict about her heart.

There was a pause. Anderson picked up the revolver beside Fleming's body and examined it swiftly, careful not to confuse his own fingerprints with any that might already be on the polished steel. Then he looked at Dale. "Who is he?" he said bluntly.

Dale fought hysteria for some seconds before she could speak.

"Richard Fleming—somebody shot him!" she managed to whisper at last.

Anderson took a step toward her.

"What do you mean by somebody?" he said.

The world to Dale turned into a crowd of threatening, accusing eyes—a multitude of shadowy voices, shouting, *Guilty! Guilty! Prove that you're innocent—you can't!*

"I don't know," she said wildly. "Somebody on the staircase."

"Did you see anybody?" Anderson's voice was as passionless and cold as a bar of steel.

"No—but there was a light from somewhere—like a pocket-flash—" She could not go on. She saw Fleming's face before her, furious at first, then changing to that strange look of bewildered, surprise. She put her hands over her eyes to shut the vision out.

Lizzie made a welcome interruption.

"I *told* you I saw a man go up that staircase!" she wailed, jabbing her forefinger in the direction of the alcove stairs.

Miss Cornelia, now recovered from the first shock of the discovery, supported her gallantly.

"That's the only explanation, Mr. Anderson," she

133

said decidedly.

The detective looked at the stairs—at the terrace door. His eyes made a circuit of the room and came back to Fleming's body. "I've been all over the house," he said. "There's nobody there."

A pause followed. Dale found herself helplessly looking toward her lover for comfort—comfort he could not give without revealing his own secret.

Eerily, through the tense silence, a sudden tinkling sounded—the sharp, persistent ringing of a telephone bell.

Miss Cornelia rose to answer it automatically. "The house phone!" she said. Then she stopped. "But we're all *here!*"

They looked at each other aghast. It was true. And yet, somehow—somewhere—one of the other phones on the circuit was calling the living-room.

Miss Cornelia summoned every ounce of inherited Van Gorder pride she possessed and went to the phone. She took off the receiver. The ringing stopped.

"Hello—hello—" she said, while the others stood rigid, listening. Then she gasped. An expression of wondering horror came over her face.

Chapter Ten: The Phone Call From Nowhere

"Somebody groaning!" gasped Miss Cornelia. "It's horrible!"

The detective stepped up and took the receiver from her. He listened anxiously for a moment.

"I don't hear anything," he said.

"*I* heard it! I couldn't *imagine* such a dreadful sound! I tell you—somebody in this house is in terrible distress."

"Where does this phone connect?" queried Anderson practically.

Miss Cornelia made a hopeless little gesture. "Practically every room in this house!"

The detective put the receiver to his ear again.

"Just what did you hear?" he said stolidly.

Miss Cornelia's voice shook.

"Dreadful groans—and what seemed to be an inarticulate effort to speak!"

Lizzie drew her gaudy wrapper closer about her shuddering form.

"I'd go somewhere," she wailed in the voice of a

lost soul, "if only I had somewhere to go!"

Miss Cornelia quelled her with a glare and turned back to the detective.

"Won't you send these men to investigate—or go yourself?" she said, indicating Brooks and Billy.

The detective thought swiftly.

"My place is here," he said. "You two men," Brooks and Billy moved forward to take his orders, "take another look through the house. Don't leave the building, I'll want you pretty soon."

Brooks—or Jack Bailey, as we may as well call him through the remainder of this narrative— started to obey. Then his eye fell on Miss Cornelia's revolver which Anderson had taken from beside Fleming's body and still held clasped in his hand.

"If you'll give me that revolver—" he began in an offhand tone, hoping Anderson would not see through his little ruse. Once wiped clean of finger-prints, the revolver would not be such telling evidence against Dale Ogden.

But Anderson was not to be caught napping.

"That revolver will stay where it is," he said with a grim smile.

Jack Bailey knew better than to try and argue the point. He followed Billy reluctantly out of the door, giving Dale a surreptitious glance of encouragement and faith as he did so. The Japanese and he mounted to the second floor as stealthily as possible, prying into dark corners and searching unused rooms for any clue that might betray the source of the startling phone call from nowhere. But Bailey's heart was not in the search. His mind kept going back to the figure of Dale—nervous, shaken, undergoing the terrors of the third degree at Anderson's hands. She *couldn't* have shot Fleming of course, and yet, unless he and Billy found something to substantiate her story of how the killing had happened, it was her own, unsupported word against a damning mass of circumstantial evidence. He plunged with renewed vigor into his quest.

Back in the living-room, as he had feared, Anderson was subjecting Dale to a merciless interrogation.

"Now I want the *real* story!" he began with calculated brutality. "You lied before!"

"That's no tone to use! You'll only terrify her," cried Miss Cornelia indignantly. The detective paid no attention, his face had hardened, he seemed every inch the remorseless sleuthhound of the law. He turned on Miss Cornelia for a moment.

"Where were you when this happened?" he said.

"Upstairs in my room." Miss Cornelia's tones were icy.

"And you?" badgeringly, to Lizzie.

"In *my* room," said the latter pertly, "brushing Miss Cornelia's hair.

Anderson broke open the revolver and gave a swift glance at the bullet chambers.

"One shot has been fired from this revolver!"

Miss Cornelia sprang to her niece's defense.

137

"I fired it myself this afternoon," she said.

The detective regarded her with grudging admiration.

"You're a quick thinker," he said with obvious unbelief in his voice. He put the revolver down on the table.

Miss Cornelia followed up her advantage.

"I demand that you get the coroner here," she said.

"Doctor Wells is the coroner," offerred Lizzie eagerly. Anderson brushed their suggestions aside.

"I'm going to ask you some questions!" he said menacingly to Dale.

But Miss Cornelia stuck to her guns. Dale was not going to be bullied into any sort of confession, true or false, if she could help it—and from the way that the girl's eyes returned with fascinated horror to the ghastly heap on the floor that had been Fleming, she knew that Dale was on the edge of violent hysteria.

"Do you mind covering that body first?" she asked crisply. The detective eyed her for a moment in a rather ugly fashion, then grunted ungraciously and, taking Fleming's raincoat from the chair, threw it over the body. Dale's eyes telegraphed her aunt a silent message of gratitude.

"Now, shall *I* telephone for the coroner?" persisted Miss Cornelia. The detective obviously resented her interference with his methods but he could not well refuse such a customary request.

"I'll do it," he said with a snort, going over to the city telephone. "What's his number?"

"He's not at his office; he's at the Johnsons'," murmured Dale.

Miss Cornelia took the telephone from Anderson's hands.

"I'll get the Johnsons', Mr. Anderson," she said firmly. The detective seemed about to rebuke her. Then his manner recovered some of its former suavity. He relinquished the telephone and turned back toward his prey.

"Now, what was Fleming doing here?" he asked Dale in a gentler voice.

Should she tell him the truth? No—Jack Bailey's safety was too inextricably bound up with the whole sinister business. She must lie, and lie again, while there was any chance of a lie's being believed.

"I don't know," she said weakly, trying to avoid the detective's eyes.

Anderson took thought.

"Well, I'll ask that question another way," he said. "How did he get into the house?"

Dale brightened—no need for a lie here.

"He had a key."

"Key to what door?"

"That door over there." Dale indicated the terrace door of the alcove.

The detective was about to ask another question—then he paused. Miss Cornelia was talking on the phone.

"Hello—is that Mr. Johnson's residence? Is Doctor Wells there? No?" Her expression was puzzled. "Oh—all right—thank you—good night—"

Meanwhile Anderson had been listening—but thinking as well. Dale saw his sharp glance travel over to the fireplace—rest for a moment, with an air of discovery, on the fragments of the roll of blueprints that remained unburned among ashes—return. She shut her eyes for a moment, trying tensely to summon every atom of shrewdness she possessed to aid her.

He was hammering her with questions again.

"When did you take the revolver out of the table drawer?"

"When I heard him outside on the terrace," said Dale promptly and truthfully. "I was frightened."

Lizzie tiptoed over to Miss Cornelia.

"You wanted a detective!" she said in an ironic whisper. "I hope you're happy now you've got one!"

Miss Cornelia gave her a look that sent her scuttling back to her former post by the door. But nevertheless, internally, she felt thoroughly in accord with Lizzie.

Again Anderson's questions pounded at the rigid Dale, striving to pierce her armor of mingled truth and falsehood.

"When Fleming came in, what did he say to you?"

"Just—something about the weather," said Dale weakly. The whole scene was still too horribly vivid

140

before her eyes for her to furnish a more convincing alibi.

"You didn't have any quarrel with him?"

Dale hesitated.

"No."

"He just came in that door, said something about the weather, and was shot from that staircase. Is that it?" said the detective in tones of utter incredulity.

Dale hesitated again. Thus baldly put, her story seemed too flimsy for words; she could not even blame Anderson for disbelieving it. And yet — what other story could she tell that would not bring ruin on Jack?

Her face whitened. She put her hand on the back of a chair for support.

"Yes — that's it," she said at last, and swayed where she stood.

Again Miss Cornelia tried to come to the rescue.

"Are all these questions necessary?" she queried sharply. "You can't for a moment believe that Miss Ogden shot that man!" But by now, though she did not show it, she too began to realize the strength of the appalling net of circumstances that drew with each minute tighter around the unhappy girl. Dale gratefully seized the momentary respite and sank into a chair. The detective looked at her.

"I think she knows more than she's telling. She's concealing something!" he said with deadly intentness. "The nephew of the president of the Union

141

Bank—shot in his own house the day the bank has failed—that's queer enough—" Now he turned back to Miss Cornelia. "But when the only person present at his murder is the girl who's engaged to the guilty cashier," he continued, watching Miss Cornelia's face as the full force of his words sank into her mind, "I want to know more about it!"

He stopped. His right hand moved idly over the edge of the table, halted beside an ash tray, closed upon something.

Miss Cornelia rose.

"Is that true, Dale?" she said sorrowfully.

Dale nodded. "Yes." She could not trust herself to explain at greater length.

Then Miss Cornelia made one of the most magnificent gestures of her life.

"Well, even if it is—what has *that* got to do with it?" she said, turning upon Anderson fiercely, all her protective instinct for those whom she loved aroused.

Anderson seemed somewhat impressed by the fierceness of her query. When he went on it was with less harshness in his manner.

"I'm not accusing this girl," he said more gently. "But behind every crime there is a motive. When we've found the motive for *this* crime, we'll have found the criminal."

Unobserved, Dale's hand instinctively went to her bosom. There it lay—the motive—the precious fragment of blueprint which she had torn from Flem-

142

ing's grasp but an instant before he was shot down. Once Anderson found it in her possession the case was closed, the evidence against her overwhelming. She could not destroy it—it was the only clue to the Hidden Room and the truth that might clear Jack Bailey. But, somehow, she must hide it—get it out of her hands—before Anderson's third-degree methods broke her down or he insisted on a search of her person. Her eyes roved wildly about the room, looking for a hiding place.

The rain of Anderson's questions began anew.

"What papers did Fleming burn in that grate?" he asked abruptly, turning back to Dale.

"Papers!" she faltered.

"Papers! The ashes are still there."

Miss Cornelia made an unavailing interruption.

"Miss Ogden has said he didn't come into this room."

The detective smiled.

"I hold in my hand proof that he was in this room for some time," he said coldly, displaying the half-burned cigarette he had taken from the ash tray a moment before.

"His cigarette—with his monogram on it." He put the fragment of tobacco and paper carefully away in an envelope and marched over to the fireplace. There he rummaged among the ashes for a moment, like a dog uncovering a bone. He returned to the center of the room with a fragment of blackened blue paper fluttering between his fingers.

"A fragment of what is technically known as a blueprint," he announced. "What were you and Richard Fleming doing with a blueprint?" His eyes bored into Dale's.

Dale hesitated—shut her lips.

"Now think it over!" he warned. "The truth will come out, sooner or later! Better to be frank *now!*

If he only knew how I wanted *to be, he wouldn't be so cruel,* thought Dale wearily. *But I can't—I can't!* Then her heart gave a throb of relief. Jack had come back into the room—Jack and Billy—Jack would protect her! But even as she thought of this her heart sank again. Protect her, indeed! Poor Jack! He would find it hard enough to protect himself if once this terrible man with the cold smile and steely eyes started questioning him. She looked up anxiously.

Bailey made his report breathlessly.

"Nothing in the house, sir."

Billy's impassive lips confirmed him.

"We go all over house—nobody!"

Nobody—nobody in the house! And yet—the mysterious ringing of the phone—the groans Miss Cornelia had heard! Were old wives' tales and witches' fables true after all? Did a power—merciless—evil—exist, outside the barriers of the flesh—blasting that trembling flesh with a cold breath from beyond the portals of the grave? There seemed to be no other explanation.

"You men stay here!" said the detective. "I want

144

to ask you some questions." He doggedly returned to his third-degreeing of Dale.

"Now what about this blueprint?" he queried sharply.

Dale stiffened in her chair. Her lies had failed. Now she would tell a portion of the truth, as much of it as she could without menacing Jack.

"I'll tell you just what happened," she began. "I sent for Richard Fleming—and when he came, I asked him if he knew where there were any blueprints of the house."

The detective pounced eagerly upon her admission.

"Why did you want blueprints?" he thundered.

"Because," Dale took a long breath, "I believe old Mr. Fleming took the money himself from the Union Bank and hid it here."

"Where did you get that idea?"

Dale's jaw set. "I won't tell you."

"What had the blueprints to do with it?"

She could think of no plausible explanation but the true one.

"Because I'd heard there was a Hidden Room in this house."

The detective leaned forward intently.

"Did you locate that room?"

Dale hesitated. "No."

"Then why did you burn the blueprints?"

Dale's nerve was crumbling—breaking—under the repeated, monotonous impact of his questions.

"He burned them!" she cried wildly. "I don't *know* why!"

The detective paused an instant, then returned to a previous query.

"Then you *didn't* locate this Hidden Room?"

Dale's lips formed a pale "No."

"Did he?" went on Anderson inexorably.

Dale stared at him, dully—the breaking point had come. Another question—another—and she would no longer be able to control herself. She would sob out the truth hysterically—that Brooks, the gardener, was Jack Bailey, the missing cashier—that the scrap of blueprint hidden in the bosom of her dress might unravel the secret of the Hidden Room— that—

But just as she felt herself, sucked of strength, beginning to slide toward a black, tingling pit of merciful oblivion, Miss Cornelia provided a diversion.

"What's that?" she said in a startled voice.

The detective turned away from his quarry for an instant.

"What's what?"

"I heard something," averred Miss Cornelia, staring toward the French windows.

All eyes followed the direction of her stare. There was an instant of silence.

Then, suddenly, traveling swiftly from right to left across the shades of the French windows, there appeared a glowing circle of brilliant white light.

Inside the circle was a black, distorted shadow—a shadow like the shadow of a gigantic black Bat! It was there—then a second later, it was gone!

"Oh, my God!" wailed Lizzie from her corner. "It's the Bat—that's his sign!"

Jack Bailey made a dash for the terrace door. But Miss Cornelia halted him peremptorily.

"Wait, Brooks!" She turned to the detective. "Mr. Anderson, you are familiar with the sign of the Bat. Did that look like it?"

The detective seemed both puzzled and disturbed.

"Well, it looked like the shadow of a bat. I'll say that for it," he said finally.

On the heels of his words the front door bell began to ring. All turned in the direction of the hall.

"I'll answer that!" said Jack Bailey eagerly.

Miss Cornelia gave him the key to the front door.

"Don't admit anyone till you know who it is," she said. Bailey nodded and disappeared into the hall. The others waited tensely. Miss Cornelia's hand crept toward the revolver lying on the table where Anderson had put it down.

There was the click of an opening door, the noise of a little scuffle, then men's voices raised in an angry dispute. "What do I know about a flashlight?" cried an irritated voice. "I haven't got a pocket-flash. Take your hands off me!" Bailey's voice answered the other voice, grim, threatening. The scuffle resumed.

147

Then Doctor Wells burst suddenly into the room, closely followed by Bailey. The doctor's tie was askew, he looked ruffled and enraged. Bailey followed him vigilantly, seeming not quite sure whether to allow him to enter or not.

"My dear Miss Van Gorder," began the doctor in tones of high dudgeon, "won't you instruct your servants that even if I do make a late call, I am not to be received with violence?"

"I asked you if you had a pocket-flash about you!" answered Bailey indignantly. "If you call a question like that violence—" He seemed about to restrain the doctor by physical force.

Miss Cornelia quelled the teapot-tempest.

"It's all right, Brooks," she said, taking the front door key from his hand and putting it back on the table. She turned to Doctor Wells.

"You see, Doctor Wells," she explained, "just a moment before you rang the doorbell a circle of white light was thrown on those window shades."

The doctor laughed with a certain relief.

"Why, that was probably the searchlight from my car!" he said. "I noticed as I drove up that it fell directly on that window."

His explanation seemed to satisfy all present but Lizzie. She regarded him with a deep suspicion. *He may be a lawyer, a merchant, a* DOCTOR, she chanted ominously to herself.

Miss Cornelia, too, was not entirely at ease.

"In the center of this ring of light," she pro-

148

ceeded, her eyes on the doctor's calm countenance, "was an almost perfect silhouette of a bat."

"A bat!" The doctor seemed at sea. "Ah, I see—the symbol of the criminal of that name." He laughed again.

"I think I can explain what you saw. Quite often my headlights collect insects at night and a large moth, spread on the glass, would give precisely the effect you speak of. Just to satisfy you, I'll go out and take a look."

He turned to do so. Then he caught sight of the raincoat-covered huddle on the floor.

"Why—" he said in a voice that mingled astonishment with horror. He paused. His glance slowly traversed the circle of silent faces.

Chapter Eleven: Billy Practices Jiu-Jitsu

"We have had a very sad occurrence here, Doctor," said Miss Cornelia gently.

The doctor braced himself.

"Who?"

"Richard Fleming."

"Richard Fleming?" gasped the doctor in tones of incredulous horror.

"Shot and killed from that staircase," said Miss Cornelia tonelessly.

The detective demurred.

"Shot and killed, anyhow," he said in accents of significant omission.

The doctor knelt beside the huddle on the floor. He removed the fold of the raincoat that covered the face of the corpse and stared at the dead, blank mask. Till a moment ago, even at the height of his irritation with Bailey, he had been blithe and off-hand—a man who seemed comparatively young for his years. Now Age seemed to fall upon him, suddenly, like a gray, clinging dust—he looked stricken and feeble under the impact of this unexpected shock.

"Shot and killed from that stairway," he repeated dully. He rose from his knees and glanced at the fatal stairs.

"What was Richard Fleming doing in this house at this hour?" he said.

He spoke to Miss Cornelia but Anderson answered the question.

"That's what *I'm* trying to find out," he said with a saturnine smile.

The doctor gave him a look of astonished inquiry. Miss Cornelia remembered her manners.

"Doctor, this is Mr. Anderson."

"Headquarters," said Anderson tersely, shaking hands.

It was Lizzie's turn to play her part in the tangled game of mutual suspicion that by now made each member of the party at Cedarcrest watch every other member with nervous distrust. She crossed to her mistress on tiptoe.

"Don't you let him fool you with any of that moth business!" she said in a thrilling whisper, jerking her thumb in the direction of the doctor. "He's the Bat."

Ordinarily Miss Cornelia would have dismissed her words with a smile. But by now her brain felt as if it had begun to revolve like a pinwheel in her efforts to fathom the uncanny mystery of the various events of the night.

She addressed Doctor Wells.

"I didn't tell you, Doctor. I sent for a detective

this afternoon." Then, with mounting suspicion, "You happened in very opportunely!"

"After I left the Johnsons' I felt very uneasy," he explained. "I determined to make one more effort to get you away from this house. As this shows, my fears were justified!"

He shook his head sadly. Miss Cornelia sat down. His last words had given her food for thought. She wanted to mull them over for a moment.

The doctor removed muffler and topcoat, stuffed the former in his topcoat pocket and threw the latter on the settee. He took out his handkerchief and began to mop his face, as if to wipe away some strain of mental excitement under which he was laboring. His breath came quickly, the muscles of his jaw stood out.

"Died instantly, I suppose?" he said, looking over at the body. "Didn't have time to say anything?"

"Ask the young lady," said Anderson, with a jerk of his head. "She was here when it happened."

The doctor gave Dale a feverish glance of inquiry.

"He just fell over," said the latter pitifully. Her answer seemed to relieve the doctor of some unseen weight on his mind. He drew a long breath and turned back toward Fleming's body with comparative calm.

"Poor Dick has proved my case for me better than I expected," he said, regarding the still, unbreathing heap beneath the raincoat. He swerved toward the detective.

"Mr. Anderson," he said with dignified pleading, "I ask you to use your influence to see that these two ladies find some safer spot than this for the night."

Lizzie bounced up from her chair, instanter.

"Two?" she wailed. "If you know any safe spot, lead me to it!"

The doctor overlooked her sudden eruption into the scene. He wandered back again toward the huddle under the raincoat, as if still unable to believe that it was—or rather had been—Richard Fleming.

Miss Cornelia spoke suddenly in a low voice, without moving a muscle of her body.

"I have a strange feeling that I'm being watched by unfriendly eyes," she said.

Lizzie clutched at her across the table.

"I wish the light would go out again!" she pattered. "No, I don't neither!" as Miss Cornelia gave the clutching hand a nervous little slap.

During the little interlude of comedy, Billy, the Japanese, unwatched by the others, had stolen into the French windows, pulled aside a blind, looked out. When he turned back to the room his face had lost a portion of its Oriental calm—there was suspicion in his eyes. Softly, under cover of pretending to arrange the tray of food that lay untouched on the table, he possessed himself of the key to the front door, unperceived by the rest, and slipped out of the room like a ghost.

Meanwhile the detective confronted Doctor Wells.

"You say, Doctor, that you came back to take these women away from the house. Why?"

The doctor gave him a dignified stare.

"Miss Van Gorder has already explained."

Miss Cornelia elucidated. "Mr. Anderson has already formed a theory of the crime," she said with a trace of sarcasm in her tones.

The detective turned on her quickly. "I haven't said that." He started.

It had come again — tinkling — persistent — the phone call from nowhere — the ringing of the bell of the house telephone!

"The house telephone — again!" breathed Dale. Miss Cornelia made a movement to answer the tinkling, inexplicable bell. But Anderson was before her.

"I'll answer that!" he barked. He sprang to the phone.

"Hello — hello —"

All eyes were bent on him nervously — the doctor's face, in particular, seemed a very study in fear and amazement. He clutched the back of a chair to support himself, his hand was the trembling hand of a sick, old man.

"Hello — hello —" Anderson swore impatiently. He hung up the phone.

"There's nobody there!"

Again a chill breath from another world than ours seemed to brush across the faces of the little group in the living-room. Dale, sensitive, impres-

154

sionable, felt a cold, uncanny prickling at the roots of her hair.

A light came into Anderson's eyes. "Where's that Jap?" he almost shouted.

"He just went out," said Miss Cornelia. The cold fear, the fear of the unearthly, subsided from around Dale's heart, leaving her shaken but more at peace.

The detective turned swiftly to the doctor, as if to put his case before the eyes of an unprejudiced witness.

"That Jap rang the phone," he said decisively. "Miss Van Gorder believes that this murder is the culmination of the series of mysterious happenings that caused her to send for me. I do not."

"Then what is the significance of the anonymous letters?" broke in Miss Cornelia heatedly. "Of the man Lizzie saw going up the stairs, of the attempt to break into this house — of the ringing of that telephone bell?"

Anderson replied with one deliberate word.

"Terrorization," he said.

The doctor moistened his dry lips in an effort to speak.

"By whom?" he asked.

Anderson's voice was an icicle.

"I imagine by Miss Van Gorder's servants. By that woman there—" he pointed at Lizzie, who rose indignantly to deny the charge. But he gave her no time for denial. He rushed on, "—who probably writes the letters," he continued. "By the gardener—" his pointing finger found Bailey "— who may have been the man Lizzie saw slipping up the stairs. By the Jap, who goes out and rings the telephone," he concluded triumphantly.

Miss Cornelia seemed unimpressed by his fervor. "With what object?" she queried smoothly.

"That's what I'm going to find out!" There was determination in Anderson's reply.

Miss Cornelia sniffed. "Absurd! The butler was in this room when the telephone rang for the first time."

The thrust pierced Anderson's armor. For once he seemed at a loss. Here was something he had omitted from his calculations. But he did not give up. He was about to retort when—crash! thud!—the noise of a violent struggle in the hall outside drew all eyes to the hall door.

An instant later the door slammed open and a disheveled young man in evening clothes was catapulted into the living-room as if slung there by a giant's arm. He tripped and fell to the floor in the center of the room. Billy stood in the doorway behind him, inscrutable, arms folded, on his face an expression of mild satisfaction as if he were demurely pleased with a neat piece of housework, neatly carried out.

The young man picked himself up, brushed off his clothes, sought for his hat, which had rolled under the table. Then he turned on Billy furiously.

"Damn you—what do you mean by this?"

"Jiu-jitsu," said Billy, his yellow face quite untroubled. "Pretty good stuff. Found on terrace with searchlight," he added.

"With searchlight?" barked Anderson.

The young man turned to face this new enemy.

"Well, why shouldn't I be on the terrace with a searchlight?" he demanded.

The detective moved toward him menacingly.

"Who *are* you?"

"Who are you?" said the young man with cool impertinence, giving him stare for stare.

Anderson did not deign to reply, in so many words. Instead he displayed the police badge which glittered on the inside of the right lapel of his coat.

The young man examined it coolly.

"H'm," he said. "Very pretty—nice neat design— very chaste!" He took out a cigarette case and opened it, seemingly entirely unimpressed by both the badge and Anderson. The detective chafed.

"If you've finished admiring my badge," he said with heavy sarcasm, "I'd like to know what you were doing on the terrace."

The young man hesitated—shot an odd, swift glance at Dale who, ever since his abrupt entrance into the room, had been sitting rigid in her chair with her hands clenched tightly together.

"I've had some trouble with my car down the road," he said finally. He glanced at Dale again. "I came to ask if I might telephone."

157

"Did it require a flashlight to find the house?" Miss Cornelia asked suspiciously.

"Look here," the young man blustered, "why are you asking me all these questions?" He tapped his cigarette case with an irritated air.

Miss Cornelia stepped closer to him.

"Do you mind letting me see that flashlight?" she said.

The young man gave it to her with a little, mocking bow. She turned it over, examined it, passed it to Anderson, who examined it also, seeming to devote particular attention to the lens. The young man stood puffing his cigarette a little nervously while the examination was in progress. He did not look at Dale again.

Anderson handed back the flashlight to its owner.

"Now—what's your name?" he said sternly.

"Beresford—Reginald Beresford," said the young man sulkily. "If you doubt it I've probably got a card somewhere—" He began to search through his pockets.

"What's your business?" went on the detective.

"What's my business here?" queried the young man, obviously fending with his interrogator.

"No, how do you earn your living?" said Anderson sharply.

"I don't," said the young man flippantly. "I may have to begin now, if that is any interest to you. As a matter of fact, I've studied law but—"

The one word was enough to start Lizzie off on

158

another trail of distrust. *He may be a* LAWYER — she quoted to herself sepulchrally from the evening newspaper article that had dealt with the mysterious identity of the Bat.

"And you came here to telephone about your car?" persisted the detective.

Dale rose from her chair with a hopeless little sigh.

"Oh, don't you see — he's trying to protect me," she said wearily. She turned to the young man. "It's no use, Mr. Beresford."

Beresford's air of flippancy vanished.

"I see," he said. He turned to the other, frankly. "Well, the plain truth is — I didn't know the situation and I thought I'd play safe for Miss Ogden's sake."

Miss Cornelia moved over to her niece protectingly. She put a hand on Dale's shoulder to reassure her. But Dale was quite composed now. She had gone through so many shocks already that one more or less seemed to make very little difference to her overwearied nerves. She turned to Anderson calmly.

"He doesn't know anything about — this," she said, indicating Beresford. "He brought Mr. Fleming here in his car — that's all."

Anderson looked to Beresford for confirmation.

"Is that true?"

"Yes," said Beresford. He started to explain. "I got tired of waiting and so I — "

159

The detective broke in curtly.

"All right."

He took a step toward the alcove.

"Now, Doctor." He nodded at the huddle beneath the raincoat. Beresford followed his glance—and saw the ominous heap for the first time.

"What's that?" he said tensely. No one answered him. The doctor was already on his knees beside the body, drawing the raincoat gently aside. Beresford stared at the shape thus revealed with frightened eyes. The color left his face.

"That's not—Dick Fleming—is it?" he said thickly. Anderson slowly nodded his head. Beresford seemed unable to believe his eyes.

"If you've looked over the ground," said the doctor in a low voice to Anderson, "I'll move the body where we can have a better light." His right hand fluttered swiftly over Fleming's still, clenched fist— extracted from it a torn corner of paper.

Still Beresford did not seem to be able to take in what had happened. He took another step toward the body.

"Do you mean to say that Dick Fleming—" he began. Anderson silenced him with an uplifted hand.

"What have you got there, Doctor?" he said in a still voice.

The doctor, still on his knees beside the corpse, lifted his head.

"What do you mean?"

160

"You took something, just then, out of Fleming's hand," said the detective.

"I took nothing out of his hand," said the doctor firmly.

Anderson's manner grew peremptory.

"I warn you not to obstruct the course of justice!" he said forcibly. "Give it here!"

The doctor rose slowly, dusting off his knees. His eyes tried to meet Anderson's and failed. He produced a torn corner of blueprint.

"Why, it's only a scrap of paper, nothing at all," he said evasively.

Anderson looked at him meaningly.

"Scraps of paper are sometimes very important," he said with a side glance at Dale.

Beresford approached the two angrily.

"Look here!" he burst out, "I've got a right to know about this thing. I brought Fleming over here and I want to know what happened to him!"

"You don't have to be a mind reader to know that!" moaned Lizzie, overcome.

As usual, her comment went unanswered. Beresford persisted in his questions.

"Who killed him? That's what *I* want to know!" he continued, nervously puffing his cigarette.

"Well, you're not alone in that," said Anderson in his grimly humorous vein.

The doctor motioned nervously to them both.

"As the coroner, if Mr. Anderson is satisfied, I suggest that the body be taken where I can make a thorough examination," he said haltingly.

Once more Anderson bent over the shell that had been Richard Fleming. He turned the body half-over — let it sink back on its face. For a moment he glanced at the corner of the blueprint in his hand, then at the doctor. Then he stood aside.

"All right," he said laconically.

So Richard Fleming left the room where he had been struck down so suddenly and strangely — borne out by Beresford, the doctor, and Jack Bailey. The little procession moved as swiftly and softly as circumstances would permit; Anderson followed its passage with watchful eyes. Billy went mechanically to pick up the stained rug which the detective had kicked aside and carried it off after the body. When the burden and its bearers, with Anderson in the rear, reached the doorway into the hall, Lizzie shrank before the sight, affrighted, and turned toward the alcove while Miss Cornelia stared unseeingly out toward the front windows. So, for perhaps a dozen ticks of time Dale was left unwatched; she made the most of her opportunity.

Her fingers fumbled at the bosom of her dress — she took out the precious, dangerous fragment of blueprint that Anderson must not find in her possession — but where to hide it, before her chance had passed? Her eyes fell on the bread roll that had fallen from the detective's supper tray to the floor when Lizzie had seen the gleaming eye on the stairs and had lain there unnoticed ever since. She bent

162

over swiftly and secreted the tantalizing scrap of blue paper in the body of the roll, smoothing the crust back above it with trembling fingers. Then she replaced the roll where it had fallen originally and straightened up just as Billy and the detective returned.

Billy went immediately to the tray, picked it up, and started to go out again. Then he noticed the roll on the floor, stooped for it, and replaced it upon the tray. He looked at Miss Cornelia for instructions.

"Take that tray out to the dining-room," she said mechanically. But Anderson's attention had already been drawn to the tiny incident.

"Wait, I'll look at that tray," he said briskly. Dale, her heart in her mouth, watched him examine the knives, the plates, even shake out the napkin to see that nothing was hidden in its folds. At last he seemed satisfied.

"All right, take it away," he commanded. Billy nodded and vanished toward the dining-room with tray and roll. Dale breathed again.

The sight of the tray had made Miss Cornelia's thoughts return to practical affairs.

"Lizzie," she commanded now, "go out in the kitchen and make some coffee. I'm sure we all need it," she sighed.

Lizzie bristled at once.

"Go out in that kitchen alone?"

"Billy's there," said Miss Cornelia wearily.

163

The thought of Billy seemed to bring little solace to Lizzie's heart.

"That Jap and his jooy-jitsu," she muttered viciously. "One twist and I'd be folded up like a pretzel."

But Miss Cornelia's manner was imperative, and Lizzie slowly dragged herself kitchenward, yawning and promising the saints repentance of every sin she had or had not committed if she were allowed to get there without something grabbing at her ankles in the dark corner of the hall.

When the door had shut behind her, Anderson turned to Dale, the corner of blueprint which he had taken from the doctor in his hand.

"Now, Miss Ogden," he said tensely, "I have here a scrap of blueprint which was in Dick Fleming's hand when he was killed. I'll trouble you for the rest of it, if you please!"

Chapter Twelve: "I Didn't Kill Him."

"The rest of it?" queried Dale with a show of bewilderment, silently thanking her stars that, for the moment at least, the incriminating fragment had passed out of her possession.

Her reply seemed only to infuriate the detective.

"Don't tell me Fleming started to go out of this house with a blank scrap of paper in his hand," he threatened. "He didn't start to go out at all!"

Dale rose. Was Anderson trying a chance shot in the dark — or had he stumbled upon some fresh evidence against her? She could not tell from his manner.

"Why do you say that?" she feinted.

"His cap's there on the table," said the detective with crushing terseness. Dale started. She had not remembered the cap — why hadn't she burned it, concealed it — as she had concealed the blueprint? She passed a hand over her forehead wearily.

Miss Cornelia watched her niece.

"If you're keeping anything back, Dale — tell

him," she said.

"She's keeping something back all right," he said. "She's told part of the truth, but not all." He hammered at Dale again. "You and Fleming located that room by means of a blueprint of the house. He started — *not* to go out — but, probably, to go up that staircase. And he had in his hand the rest of this!" Again he displayed the blank corner of blue paper.

Dale knew herself cornered at last. The detective's deductions were too shrewd; do what she would, she could keep him away from the truth no longer.

"He was going to take the money and go away with it!" she said rather pitifully, feeling a certain relief of despair steal over her, now that she no longer needed to go on lying — lying — involving herself in an inextricable web of falsehood.

"Dale!" gasped Miss Cornelia, alarmed. But Dale went on, reckless of consequences to herself, though still warily shielding Jack.

"He changed the minute he heard about it. He was all kindness before that — but afterward —" She shuddered, closing her eyes. Fleming's face rose before her again, furious, distorted with passion and greed — then, suddenly, quenched of life.

Anderson turned to Miss Cornelia triumphantly.

"She started to find the money — and save Bailey," he explained, building up his theory of the crime. "But to do it she had to take Fleming into her confidence — and he turned yellow. Rather than let him get away with it, she—" He made an expressive gesture toward his hip pocket.

Dale trembled, feeling herself already in the toils. She had not quite realized, until now, how damningly plausible such an explanation of Fleming's death could sound. It fitted the evidence perfectly, it took account of every factor but one—the factor left unaccounted for was one which even she herself could not explain.

"Isn't that true?" demanded Anderson. Dale already felt the cold clasp of handcuffs on her slim wrists. What use of denial when every tiny circumstance was so leagued against her? And yet she must deny.

"I didn't kill him," she repeated perplexedly, weakly.

"Why didn't you call for help? You—you knew I was here."

Dale hesitated. "I—I couldn't." The moment the words were out of her mouth she knew from his expression that they had only cemented his growing certainty of her guilt.

"Dale! Be careful what you say!" warned Miss Cornelia agitatedly. Dale looked dumbly at her aunt. Her answers must seem the height of reckless folly to Miss Cornelia—oh, if there were only someone who understood!

Anderson resumed his grilling.

"Now I mean to find out two things," he said, advancing upon Dale. "*Why* you did not call for help—and *what* you have done with that blueprint."

"Suppose I could find that piece of blueprint for you?" said Dale desperately. "Would that establish Jack Bailey's innocence?"

The detective stared at her keenly for a moment.

"If the money's there—yes."

Dale opened her lips to reveal the secret, reckless of what might follow. As long as Jack was cleared—what matter what happened to herself? But Miss Cornelia nipped the heroic attempt at self-sacrifice in the bud.

She put herself between her niece and the detective, shielding Dale from his eager gaze.

"But her own guilt!" she said in tones of great dignity. "No, Mr. Anderson, granting that she knows where that paper is—and she has not said that she does, I shall want more time and much legal advice before I allow her to turn it over to you."

All the unconscious note of command that long-inherited wealth and the pride of a great name can give was in her voice, and the detective, for the moment, bowed before it, defeated. Perhaps he thought of men who had been broken from the Force for injudicious arrests, perhaps he merely bided his time. At any rate, he gave up his grilling of Dale for the present and turned to question the doctor and Beresford who had just returned, with Jack Bailey, from their grim task of placing Fleming's body in a temporary resting place in the li-

168

brary.

"Well, Doctor?" he grunted.

The doctor shook his head.

"Poor fellow—straight through the heart."

"Were there any powder marks?" queried Miss Cornelia.

"No—and the clothing was not burned. He was apparently shot from some little distance—and I should say from above."

The detective received this information without the change of a muscle in his face. He turned to Beresford—resuming his attack on Dale from another angle.

"Beresford, did Fleming tell you why he came here tonight?"

Beresford considered the question.

"No. He seemed in a great hurry, said Miss Ogden had telephoned him, and asked me to drive him over."

"Why did you come up to the house?"

"We-el," said Beresford with seeming candor, "I thought it was putting rather a premium on friendship to keep me sitting out in the rain all night, so I came up the drive—and, by the way!" He snapped his fingers irritatedly, as if recalling some significant incident that had slipped his memory, and drew a battered object from his pocket. "I picked this up, about a hundred feet from the house," he explained. "A man's watch. It was partly crushed into the ground, and, as you see, it's stopped running."

The detective took the object and examined it carefully. A man's open-faced gold watch, crushed and battered in as if it had been trampled upon by a heavy heel.

"Yes," he said thoughtfully. "Stopped running at ten-thirty."

Beresford went on, with mounting excitement.

"I was using my pocket-flash to find my way and what first attracted my attention was the ground — torn up, you know, all around it. Then I saw the watch itself. Anybody here recognize it?"

The detective silently held up the watch so that all present could examine it. He waited. But if anyone in the party recognized the watch — no one moved forward to claim it.

"You didn't hear any evidence of a struggle, did you?" went on Beresford. "The ground looked as if a fight had taken place. Of course it might have been a dozen other things."

Miss Cornelia started.

"Just about ten-thirty Lizzie heard somebody cry out, in the grounds," she said.

The detective looked Beresford over till the latter grew a little uncomfortable.

"I don't suppose it has any bearing on the case," admitted the latter uneasily. "But it's interesting."

The detective seemed to agree. At least he slipped the watch in his pocket.

"Do you always carry a flashlight, Mr. Beresford?" asked Miss Cornelia a trifle suspiciously.

"Always at night, in the car." His reply was prompt and certain.

"This is all you found?" queried the detective, a curious note in his voice.

"Yes." Beresford sat down, relieved. Miss Cornelia followed his example. Another clue had led into a blind alley, leaving the mystery of the night's affairs as impenetrable as ever.

"Some day I hope to meet the real estate agent who promised me that I would sleep here as I never slept before!" she murmured acridly. "He's right! I've slept with my clothes on every night since I came!"

As she ended, Billy darted in from the hall, his beady little black eyes gleaming with excitement, a long, wicked-looking butcher knife in his hand.

"Key, kitchen door, please!" he said, addressing his mistress.

"Key?" said Miss Cornelia, startled. "What for?"

For once Billy's polite little grin was absent from his countenance.

"Somebody outside trying to get in," he chattered. "I see knob turn, so," he illustrated with the butcher knife, "and so—three times."

The detective's hand went at once to his revolver.

"You're sure of that, are you?" he said roughly to Billy.

"Sure, I sure!"

"Where's that hysterical woman Lizzie?" queried Anderson. "She may get a bullet in her if she's not

171

careful."

"She see too. She shut in closet—say prayers, maybe," said Billy, without a smile.

The picture was a ludicrous one but not one of the little group laughed.

"Doctor, have you a revolver?" Anderson seemed to be going over the possible means of defense against this new peril.

"No."

"How about you, Beresford?"

Beresford hesitated.

"Yes," he admitted finally. "Always carry one at night in the country." The statement seemed reasonable enough but Miss Cornelia gave him a sharp glance of mistrust, nevertheless.

The detective seemed to have more confidence in the young idler.

"Beresford, will you go with this Jap to the kitchen?" as Billy, grimly clutching his butcher knife, retraced his steps toward the hall. "If anyone's working at the knob—shoot through the door. I'm going round to take a look outside."

Beresford started to obey. Then he paused.

"I advise you not to turn the doorknob yourself, then," he said flippantly.

The detective nodded. "Much obliged," he said, with a grin. He ran lightly into the alcove and tiptoed out of the terrace door, closing the door behind him. Beresford and Billy departed to take up their posts in the kitchen. "I'll go with you, if you don't mind—" and Jack Bailey had followed them, leaving Miss Cornelia and Dale alone with the doctor. Miss Cornelia, glad of the opportunity to get the doctor's theories on the mystery without Anderson's interference, started to question him at once.

"Doctor."

"Yes." The doctor turned, politely.

"Have *you* any theory about this occurrence tonight?" She watched him eagerly as she asked the question.

He made a gesture of bafflement.

"None whatever, it's beyond me," he confessed.

"And yet you warned me to leave this house," said Miss Cornelia cannily. "You didn't have any reason to believe that the situation was even as serious as it has proved to be?"

"I did the perfectly obvious thing when I warned you," said the doctor easily. "Those letters made a distinct threat."

Miss Cornelia could not deny the truth in his words. And yet she felt decidedly unsatisfied with the way things were progressing.

"You said Fleming had probably been shot from above?" she queried, thinking hard.

The doctor nodded. "Yes."

"Have you a pocket-flash, Doctor?" she asked him suddenly.

"Why—yes—" The doctor did not seem to perceive the significance of the query. "A flashlight is more important to a country doctor than—castor

173

oil," he added, with a little smile.

Miss Cornelia decided upon an experiment. She turned to Dale.

"Dale, you said you saw a white light shining down from above?"

"Yes," said Dale in a minor voice.

Miss Cornelia rose.

"May I borrow your flashlight, Doctor? Now that fool detective is out of the way," she continued somewhat acidly, "I want to do something."

The doctor gave her his flashlight with a stare of bewilderment. She took it and moved into the alcove.

"Doctor, I shall ask you to stand at the foot of the small staircase, facing up."

"Now?" queried the doctor with some reluctance.

"Now, please."

The doctor slowly followed her into the alcove and took up the position she assigned him at the foot of the stairs.

"Now, Dale," said Miss Cornelia briskly, "when I give the word, you put out the lights here—and then tell me when I have reached the point on the staircase from which the flashlight seemed to come. All ready?"

Two silent nods gave assent. Miss Cornelia left the room to seek the second floor by the main staircase and then slowly return by the alcove stairs, her flashlight poised, in her reconstruction of the events of the crime. At the foot of the alcove stairs the doctor waited uneasily for her arrival. He glanced up the stairs — were those her footsteps now? He peered more closely into the darkness.

An expression of surprise and apprehension came over his face.

He glanced swiftly at Dale — was she watching him? No — she sat in her chair, musing. He turned back toward the stairs and made a frantic, insistent gesture — "Go back, go back!" it said, plainer than words, to — Something — in the darkness by the head of the stairs. Then his face relaxed, he gave a noiseless sigh of relief.

Dale, rousing from her brown study, turned out the floor lamp by the table and went over to the main light switch, awaiting Miss Cornelia's signal to plunge the room in darkness. The doctor stole another glance at her — had his gestures been observed? — apparently not.

Unobserved by either, as both waited tensely for Miss Cornelia's signal, a Hand stole through the broken pane of the shattered French window behind their backs and fumbled for the knob which unlocked the window-door. It found the catch — unlocked it — the window-door swung open, noiselessly — just enough to admit a crouching figure that cramped itself uncomfortably behind the settee which Dale and the doctor had placed to barricade those very doors. When it had settled itself, unperceived, in its lurking place — the Hand stole out again — closed the window-door, relocked it.

175

Hand or claw? Hand of man or woman or paw of beast? In the name of God—*whose hand?*

Miss Cornelia's voice from the head of the stairs broke the silence.

"All right! Put out the lights!"

Dale pressed the switch. Heavy darkness. The sound of her own breathing. A mutter from the doctor. Then, abruptly, a white, piercing shaft of light cut the darkness of the stairs—horribly reminiscent of that other light-shaft that had signaled Fleming's doom.

"Was it here?" Miss Cornelia's voice came muffledly from the head of the stairs.

Dale considered. "Come down a little," she said. The white spot of light wavered, settled on the doctor's face.

"I hope you haven't a weapon," the doctor called up the stairs with an unsuccessful attempt at jocularity.

Miss Cornelia descended another step.

"How's this?"

"That's about right," said Dale uncertainly. Miss Cornelia was satisfied.

"Lights, please." She went up the stairs again to see if she could puzzle out what course of escape the man who had shot Fleming had taken after his crime—if it had been a man.

Dale switched on the living-room lights with a sense of relief. The reconstruction of the crime had tried her sorely. She sat down to recover her poise.

176

"Doctor! I'm so frightened!" she confessed.

The doctor at once assumed his best manner of professional reassurance.

"Why, my dear child?" he asked lightly. "Because you happened to be in the room when a crime was committed?"

"But he has a perfect case against me," sighed Dale.

"That's absurd!"

"No."

"You don't mean?" said the doctor aghast.

Dale looked at him with horror in her face.

"I didn't kill him!" she insisted anew. "But, you know the piece of blueprint you found in his hand?"

"Yes," from the doctor tensely.

Dale's nerves, too bitterly tested, gave way at last under the strain of keeping her secret. She felt that she must confide in someone or perish. The doctor was kind and thoughtful—more than that, he was an experienced man of the world—if he could not advise her, who could? Besides, a doctor was in many ways like a priest—both sworn to keep inviolate the secrets of their respective confessionals.

"There was another piece of blueprint, a larger piece—" said Dale slowly, "I tore it from him just before—"

The doctor seemed greatly excited by her words. But he controlled himself swiftly.

"Why did you do such a thing?"

"Oh, I'll explain that later," said Dale tiredly, only too glad to be talking the matter out at last, to pay attention to the logic of her sentences. "It's not safe where it is," she went on, as if the doctor already knew the whole story. "Billy may throw it out or burn it without knowing—"

"Let me understand this," said the doctor. "The butler has the paper now?"

"He doesn't know he has it. It was in one of the rolls that went out on the tray."

The doctor's eyes gleamed. He gave Dale's shoulder a sympathetic pat.

"Now don't you worry about it, I'll get it," he said. Then, on the point of going toward the dining-room, he turned.

"But you oughtn't to have it in your possession," he said thoughtfully. "Why not let it be burned?"

Dale was on the defensive at once.

"Oh, no! It's important, it's vital!" she said decidedly.

The doctor seemed to consider ways and means of getting the paper.

"The tray is in the dining-room?" he asked.

"Yes," said Dale.

He thought a moment, then left the room by the hall door. Dale sank back in her chair and felt a sense of overpowering relief steal over her whole body, as if new life had been poured into her veins. The doctor had been so helpful—why had she not confided in him before? He would know what to do with the paper; she would have the benefit of his counsel through the rest of this troubled time. For a moment she saw herself and Jack, exonerated, their worries at an end, wandering hand in hand over the green lawns of Cedarcrest in the cheerful sunlight of morning.

Behind her, mockingly, the head of the Unknown concealed behind the settee lifted cautiously until, if she had turned, she would have just been able to perceive the top of its skull.

Chapter Thirteen: The Blackened Bag

As it chanced, she did not turn. The hall door opened—the head behind the settee sank down again. Jack Bailey entered, carrying a couple of logs of firewood.

Dale moved toward him as soon as he had shut the door.

"Oh, things have gone awfully wrong, haven't they?" she said with a little break in her voice.

He put his fingers to his lips.

"Be careful!" he whispered. He glanced about the room cautiously.

"I don't trust even the furniture in this house tonight!" he said. He took Dale hungrily in his arms and kissed her once, swiftly, on the lips. Then they parted, his voice changed to the formal voice of a servant.

"Miss Van Gorder wishes the fire kept burning," he announced, with a whispered *"Play up!"* to Dale.

Dale caught his meaning at once.

"Put some logs on the fire, please," she said loudly for the benefit of any listening ears. Then in an undertone to Bailey, "Jack—I'm nearly distracted!"

Bailey threw his wood on the fire, which received it with appreciative crackles and sputterings. Then again, for a moment, he clasped his sweetheart closely to him.

"Dale, pull yourself together!" he whispered warningly. "We've got a fight ahead of us!"

He released her and turned back toward the fire.

"These old-fashioned fireplaces eat up a lot of wood," he said in casual tones, pretending to arrange the logs with the poker so the fire would draw more cleanly.

But Dale felt that she must settle one point between them before they took up their game of pretense again.

"You know why I sent for Richard Fleming, don't you?" she said, her eyes fixed beseechingly on her lover. The rest of the world might interpret her action as it pleased but she couldn't bear to have Jack misunderstand.

But there was no danger of that. His faith in her was too complete.

"Yes, of course—" he said, with a look of gratitude. Then his mind reverted to the ever-present problem before them. "But who in God's name killed him?" he muttered, kneeling before the fire.

"You don't think it was—Billy?" Dale saw Billy's

face before her for a moment, calm, impassive. But he was an Oriental, an alien; his face might be just as calm, just as impassive while his hands were still red with blood. She shuddered at the thought.

Bailey considered the matter.

"More likely the man Lizzie saw going upstairs," he said finally. "But—I've been all over the upper floors."

"And—nothing?" breathed Dale.

"Nothing." Bailey's voice had an accent of dour finality. "Dale, do you think that—" he began.

Some instinct warned the girl that they were not to continue their conversation uninterrupted. "Be careful!" she breathed, as footsteps sounded in the hall. Bailey nodded and turned back to his pretense of mending the fire. Dale moved away from him slowly.

The door opened and Miss Cornelia entered, her black knitting-bag in her hand, on her face a demure little smile of triumph. She closed the door carefully behind her and began to speak at once.

"Well, Mr. Alopecia—Urticaria—Rubeola—otherwise *Bailey!*" she said in tones of the greatest satisfaction, addressing herself to Bailey's rigid back. Bailey jumped to his feet mechanically at her mention of his name. He and Dale exchanged one swift and hopeless glance of utter defeat.

"I wish," proceeded Miss Cornelia, obviously enjoying the situation to the full, "I wish you young people would remember that even if hair and teeth

182

have fallen out at sixty the mind still functions."

She pulled out a cabinet photograph from the depths of her knitting-bag.

"His photograph—sitting on your dresser!" she chided Dale. "Burn it and be quick about it!"

Dale took the photograph but continued to stare at her aunt with incredulous eyes.

"Then—you knew?" she stammered.

Miss Cornelia, the effective little tableau she had planned now accomplished to her most humorous satisfaction, relapsed into a chair.

"My dear child," said the indomitable lady, with a sharp glance at Bailey's bewildered face, "I have employed many gardeners in my time and never before had one who manicured his fingernails, wore silk socks, and regarded baldness as a plant instead of a calamity."

An unwilling smile began to break on the faces of both Dale and her lover. The former crossed to the fireplace and threw the damning photograph of Bailey on the flames. She watched it shrivel, curl up, be reduced to ash. She stirred the ashes with a poker till they were well scattered.

Bailey, recovering from the shock of finding that Miss Cornelia's sharp eyes had pierced his disguise without his even suspecting it, now threw himself on her mercy.

"Then you know why I'm here?" he stammered.

"I still have a certain amount of imagination! I may think you are a fool for taking the risk, but I

183

can see what that idiot of a detective might not—that if you had looted the Union Bank you wouldn't be trying to discover if the money is in this house. You would at least presumably know where it is."

The knowledge that he had an ally in this brisk and indomitable spinster lady cheered him greatly. But she did not wait for any comment from him. She turned abruptly to Dale.

"Now I want to ask *you* something," she said more gravely. "Was there a blueprint, and did you get it from Richard Fleming?"

It was Dale's turn now to bow her head.

"Yes," she confessed.

Bailey felt a thrill of horror run through him. She hadn't told him this!

"Dale!" he said uncomprehendingly, "don't you see where this places you? If you had it, why didn't you give it to Anderson when he asked for it?"

"Because," said Miss Cornelia uncompromisingly, "she had sense enough to see that Mr. Anderson considered that piece of paper the final link in the evidence against *her!*"

"But she could have no *motive!*" stammered Bailey, distraught, still failing to grasp the significance of Dale's refusal.

"Couldn't she?" queried Miss Cornelia pityingly. "The detective thinks she could—to save you!"

Now the full light of revelation broke upon Bailey. He took a step back.

"Good God!" he said.

Miss Cornelia would have liked to comment tartly upon the singular lack of intelligence displayed by even the nicest young men in trying circumstances. But there was no time. They might be interrupted at any moment and before they were, there were things she must find out.

"Where is that paper, now?" she asked Dale sharply.

"Why—the doctor is getting it for me." Dale seemed puzzled by the intensity of her aunt's manner.

"What?" almost shouted Miss Cornelia. Dale explained.

"It was on the tray Billy took out," she said, still wondering why so simple an answer should disturb Miss Cornelia so greatly.

"Then I'm afraid everything's over," Miss Cornelia said despairingly, and made her first gesture of defeat. She turned away. Dale followed her, still unable to fathom her course of reasoning.

"I didn't know what else to do," she said rather plaintively, wondering if again, as with Fleming, she had misplaced her confidence at a moment critical for them all.

But Miss Cornelia seemed to have no great patience with her dejection.

"One of two things will happen now," she said, with acrid logic. "Either the doctor's an honest man—in which case, as coroner, he will hand that paper to the detective." Dale gasped. "Or he is *not* an honest man," went on Miss Cornelia, "and he will keep it for himself. *I* don't think he's an honest man."

The frank expression of her distrust seemed to calm her a little. She resumed her interrogation of Dale more gently.

"Now, let's be clear about this. Had Richard Fleming ascertained that there was a concealed room in this house?"

"He was starting up to it!" said Dale in the voice of a ghost, remembering.

"Just what did you tell him?"

"That I believed there was a Hidden Room in the house and that the money from the Union Bank might be in it."

Again, for the millionth time, indeed it seemed to her, she reviewed the circumstances of the crime.

"Could anyone have overheard?" asked Miss Cornelia.

The question had rung in Dale's ears ever since she had come to her senses after the firing of the shot and seen Fleming's body stark on the floor of the alcove.

"I don't know," she said. "We were very cautious."

"You don't know where this room is?"

"No, I never saw the print. Upstairs somewhere, for he—"

"Upstairs! Then the thing to do, if we can get

186

that paper from the doctor, is to locate the room at once."

Jack Bailey did not recognize the direction where her thoughts were tending. It seemed terrible to him that anyone should devote a thought to the money while Dale was still in danger.

"What does the money matter now?" he broke in somewhat irritably. "We've got to save *her!*" and his eyes went to Dale.

Miss Cornelia gave him an ineffable look of weary patience.

"The money matters a great deal," she said, sensibly. "Someone was in this house on the same errand as Richard Fleming. After all," she went on with a tinge of irony, "the course of reasoning that you followed, Mr. Bailey, is not necessarily unique."

She rose.

"Somebody else may have suspected that Courtleigh Fleming robbed his own bank," she said thoughtfully. Her eye fell on the doctor's professional bag. She seemed to consider it as if it were a strange sort of animal.

"Find the man who followed *your* course of reasoning," she ended, with a stare at Bailey, "and you have found the murderer."

"With that reasoning you might suspect *me!*" said the latter a trifle touchily.

Miss Cornelia did not give an inch.

"I have," she said. Dale shot a swift, sympathetic glance at her lover, another less sympathetic and

187

more indignant at her aunt. Miss Cornelia smiled.

"However, I now suspect somebody else," she said. They waited for her to reveal the name of the suspect but she kept her own counsel. By now she had entirely given up confidence if not in the probity at least in the intelligence of all persons, male or female, under the age of sixty-five.

She rang the bell for Billy. But Dale was still worrying over the possible effects of the confidence she had given Doctor Wells.

"Then you think the doctor may give this paper to Mr. Anderson?" she asked.

"He may or he may not. It is entirely possible that he may elect to search for this room himself! He may even already have gone upstairs!"

She moved quickly to the door and glanced across toward the dining-room, but so far apparently all was safe. The doctor was at the table making a pretense of drinking a cup of coffee and Billy was in close attendance. That the doctor already had the paper she was certain; it was the use he intended to make of it that was her concern.

She signaled to the Jap and he came out into the hall. Beresford, she learned, was still in the kitchen with his revolver, waiting for another attempt on the door and the detective was still outside in his search. To Billy she gave her order in a low voice.

"If the doctor attempts to go upstairs," she said, "let me know at once. Don't seem to be watching. You can be in the pantry. But let me know instantly."

Once back in the living-room the vague outlines of a plan, a test, formed slowly in Miss Cornelia's mind, grew more definite.

"Dale, watch that door and warn me if anyone is coming!" she commanded, indicating the door into the hall. Dale obeyed, marveling silently at her aunt's extraordinary force of character. Most of Miss Cornelia's contemporaries would have called for a quiet ambulance to take them to a sanatorium some hours ere this. But Miss Cornelia was not merely, comparatively speaking, as fresh as a daisy; her manner bore every evidence of a firm intention to play Sherlock Holmes to the mysteries that surrounded her, in spite of doctors, detectives, dubious noises, or even the Bat himself.

The last of the Van Gorder spinsters turned to Bailey now.

"Get some soot from that fireplace," she ordered. "Be quick. Scrape it off with a knife or a piece of paper. Anything."

Bailey wondered and obeyed. As he was engaged in his grimy task, Miss Cornelia got out a piece of writing paper from a drawer and placed it on the center table, with a lead pencil beside it.

Bailey emerged from the fireplace with a handful of sooty flakes.

"Is this all right?"

"Yes. Now rub it on the handle of that bag." She indicated the little black bag in which Doctor Wells

189

carried the usual paraphernalia of a country doctor.

A private suspicion grew in Bailey's mind as to whether Miss Cornelia's fine but eccentric brain had not suffered too sorely under the shocks of the night. But he did not dare disobey. He blackened the handle of the doctor's bag with painstaking thoroughness and awaited further instructions.

"Somebody's coming!" Dale whispered, warning from her post by the door.

Bailey quickly went to the fireplace and resumed his pretended labors with the fire. Miss Cornelia moved away from the doctor's bag and spoke for the benefit of whoever might be coming.

"We all need sleep," she began, as if ending a conversation with Dale, "and I think—"

The door opened, admitting Billy.

"Doctor just go upstairs," he said, and went out again leaving the door open.

A flash passed across Miss Cornelia's face. She stepped to the door. She called.

"Doctor! Oh, Doctor!"

"Yes?" answered the doctor's voice from the main staircase. His steps clattered down the stairs; he entered the room. Perhaps he read something in Miss Cornelia's manner that demanded an explanation of his action. At any rate, he forestalled her, just as she was about to question him.

"I was about to look around above," he said. "I don't like to leave if there is the possibility of some assassin still hidden in the house."

"That is very considerate of you. But we are well protected now. And besides, why should this person remain in the house? The murder is done, the police are here."

"True," he said. "I only thought—"

But a knocking at the terrace door interrupted him. While the attention of the others was turned in that direction Dale, less cynical than her aunt, made a small plea to him and realized before she had finished with it that the doctor too had his price.

"Doctor—*did you get it?*" she repeated, drawing the doctor aside.

The doctor gave her a look of apparent bewilderment.

"My dear child," he said softly, "are you *sure* that you put it there?"

Dale felt as if she had received a blow in the face.

"Why, yes—I—" she began in tones of utter dismay. Then she stopped. The doctor's seeming bewilderment was too pat, too plausible. Of course she was sure—and, though possible, it seemed extremely unlikely that anyone else could have discovered the hiding-place of the blueprint in the few moments that had elapsed between the time when Billy took the tray from the room and the time when the doctor ostensibly went to find it. A cold wave of distrust swept over her; she turned away from the doctor silently.

Meanwhile Anderson had entered, slamming the

191

terrace-door behind him.

"I couldn't find anybody!" he said in an irritated voice. "I think that Jap's crazy."

The doctor began to struggle into his topcoat, avoiding any look at Dale.

"Well," he said, "I believe I've fulfilled all the legal requirements. I think I must be going." He turned toward the door but the detective halted him.

"Doctor," he said, "did you ever hear Courtleigh Fleming mention a Hidden Room in this house?"

If the doctor started, the movement passed apparently unnoted by Anderson. And his reply was coolly made.

"No—and I knew him rather well."

"You don't think then," persisted the detective, "that such a room and the money in it could be the motive for this crime?"

The doctor's voice grew a little curt.

"I don't believe Courtleigh Fleming robbed his own bank, if that's what you mean," he said with nicely calculated emphasis, real or feigned. He crossed over to get his bag and spoke to Miss Cornelia.

"Well, Miss Van Gorder," he said, picking up the bag by its blackened handle, "I can't wish you a comfortable night but I can wish you a quiet one."

Miss Cornelia watched him silently. As he turned to go, she spoke.

"We're all of us a little upset, naturally," she confessed. "Perhaps you could write a prescription—a sleeping-powder or a bromide of some sort."

"Why, certainly," agreed the doctor at once. He turned back. Miss Cornelia seemed pleased.

"I hoped you would," she said with a little tremble in her voice such as might easily occur in the voice of a nervous old lady. "Oh, yes, here's paper and a pencil," as the doctor fumbled in a pocket.

The doctor took the sheet of paper she proffered and, using the side of his bag as a pad, began to write out the prescription.

"I don't generally advise these drugs," he said, looking up for a moment. "Still—"

He paused. "What time is it?"

Miss Cornelia glanced at the clock. "Half-past eleven."

"Then I'd better bring you the powders myself," decided the doctor. "The pharmacy closes at eleven. I shall have to make them up myself."

"That seems a lot of trouble."

"Nothing is any trouble if I can be helpful," he assured her, smilingly. And Miss Cornelia also smiled, took the piece of paper from his hand, glanced at it once, as if out of idle curiosity about the unfinished prescription, and then laid it down on the table with a careless little gesture. Dale gave her aunt a glance of dumb entreaty. Miss Cornelia read her wish for another moment alone with the doctor.

"Dale will let you out, Doctor," said she, giving

the girl the key to the front door.

The doctor approved her watchfulness.

"That's right," he said smilingly. "Keep things locked up. Discretion is the better part of valor!"

But Miss Cornelia failed to agree with him.

"I've been discreet for sixty-five years," she said with a sniff, "and sometimes I think it was a mistake!"

The doctor laughed easily and followed Dale out of the room, with a nod of farewell to the others in passing. The detective, seeking for some object upon whom to vent the growing irritation which seemed to possess him, made Bailey the scapegoat of his wrath.

"I guess we can do without you for the present!" he said, with an angry frown at the latter. Bailey flushed, then remembered himself, and left the room submissively, with the air of a well-trained servant accepting an unmerited rebuke. The detective turned at once to Miss Cornelia.

"Now I want a few words with you!"

"Which means that you mean to do all the talking!" said Miss Cornelia acidly. "Very well! But first I want to show you something. Will you come here, please, Mr. Anderson?"

She started for the alcove.

"I've examined that staircase," said the detective.

"Not with me!" insisted Miss Cornelia. "I have something to show you."

He followed her unwillingly up the stairs, his

whole manner seeming to betray a complete lack of confidence in the theories of all amateur sleuths in general and spinster detectives of sixty-five in particular. Their footsteps died away up the alcove stairs. The living-room was left vacant for an instant.

Vacant? Only in seeming. The moment that Miss Cornelia and the detective had passed up the stairs, the crouching, mysterious Unknown, behind the settee, began to move. The French window-door opened, a stealthy figure passed through it silently to be swallowed up in the darkness of the terrace.

And poor Lizzie, entering the room at that moment, saw a hand covered with blood reach back and gropingly, horribly, through the broken pane, refasten the lock.

She shrieked madly.

195

Chapter Fourteen: Handcuffs

Dale had failed with the doctor. When Lizzie's screams once more had called the startled household to the living-room, she knew she had failed. She followed in mechanically, watched an irritated Anderson send the Pride of Kerry to bed and threaten to lock her up, and listened vaguely to the conversation between her aunt and the detective that followed it, without more than casual interest.

Nevertheless, that conversation was to have vital results later on.

"Your point about the thumbprint on the stair rail is very interesting," Anderson said with a certain respect. "But just what does it prove?"

"It points down," said Miss Cornelia, still glowing with the memory of the whistle of surprise the detective had given when she had shown him the strange thumbprint on the rail of the alcove stairs.

"It does," he admitted. "But what then?"

Miss Cornelia tried to put her case as clearly and tersely as possible.

"It shows that somebody stood there for some time, listening to my niece and Richard Fleming in this room below," she said.

"All right, I'll grant that to save argument," retorted the detective. "But the moment that shot was fired the lights came on. If somebody on that staircase shot him, and then came down and took the blueprint, Miss Ogden would have seen him."

He turned upon Dale.

"Did you?"

She hesitated. Why hadn't she thought of such an explanation before? But now—it would sound too flimsy!

"No, nobody came down," she admitted candidly.

The detective's face altered, grew menacing. Miss Cornelia once more had put herself between him and Dale.

"Now, Mr. Anderson—" she warned.

The detective was obviously trying to keep his temper.

"I'm not hounding this girl!" he said doggedly. "I haven't said yet that she committed the murder but she took that blueprint and I want it!"

"You want it to connect her with the murder," parried Miss Cornelia.

The detective threw up his hands.

"It's rather reasonable to suppose that I might want to return the funds to the Union Bank, isn't it?" he queried in tones of heavy sarcasm. "Provided they're here," he added doubtfully.

Miss Cornelia resolved upon comparative frankness.

"I see," she said. "Well, I'll tell you this much, Mr. Anderson, and I'll ask you to believe me as a lady. Granting that at one time my niece knew something of that blueprint—at this moment we do not know where it is or who has it."

Her words had the unmistakable ring of truth. The very oath from the detective that succeeded them showed his recognition of the fact.

"Damnation," he muttered. "That's true, is it?"

"That's true," said Miss Cornelia firmly. A silence of troubled thoughts fell upon the three. Miss Cornelia took out her knitting.

"Did you ever try knitting when you wanted to think?" she queried sweetly, after a pause in which the detective trampled from one side of the room to the other, brows knotted, eyes bent on the floor.

"No," grunted the detective. He took out a cigar, bit off the end with a savage snap of teeth, lit it, resumed his pacing.

"You should, sometimes," continued Miss Cornelia, watching his troubled movements with a faint light of mockery in her eyes. "I find it very helpful."

"I don't need knitting to think straight," rasped Anderson indignantly. Miss Cornelia's eyes danced.

"I wonder!" she said with caustic affability. "You seem to have so much evidence left over."

The detective paused and glared at her helplessly.

"Did you ever hear of the man who took a clock apart and when he put it together again, he had enough left over to make another clock?" she twitted.

The detective, ignoring the taunt, crossed quickly to Dale.

"What do you mean by saying that paper isn't where you put it?" he demanded in tones of extreme severity.

Miss Cornelia replied for her niece.

"She hasn't said that."

The detective made an impatient movement of his hand and walked away, as if to get out of the reach of the indefatigable spinster's tongue. But Miss Cornelia had not finished with him yet, by any means.

"Do you believe in circumstantial evidence?" she asked him with seeming ingenuousness.

"It's my business," said the detective stolidly. Miss Cornelia smiled.

"While you have been investigating," she announced, "I, too, have not been idle."

The detective gave a barking laugh. She let it pass.

"To me," she continued, "it is perfectly obvious that *one* intelligence has been at work behind many of the things that have occurred in this house."

Now Anderson observed her with a new respect.

"Who?" he grunted tersely.

Her eyes flashed.

"I'll ask you that! Some one person who, knowing Courtleigh Fleming well, probably knows of the existence of a Hidden Room in this house and who, finding us in occupation of the house, has tried to get rid of me in two ways. First, by frightening me with anonymous threats and, second, by urging me to leave. Someone, who very possibly entered this house tonight shortly before the murder and slipped up that staircase!"

The detective had listened to her outburst with unusual thoughtfulness. A certain wonder—perhaps at her shrewdness, perhaps at an unexpected confirmation of certain ideas of his own—grew upon his face. Now he jerked out two words.

"The doctor?"

Miss Cornelia knitted on as if every movement of her needles added one more link to the strong chain of probabilities she was piecing together.

"When Doctor Wells said he was leaving here earlier in the evening for the Johnsons' he did not go there," she observed. "He was not expected to go there. I found that out when I telephoned."

"The doctor!" repeated the detective, his eyes narrowing, his head beginning to sway from side to side like the head of some great cat just before a spring.

"As you know," Miss Cornelia went on, "I had a supplementary bolt placed on that terrace door today." She nodded toward the door that gave access into the alcove from the terrace. "Earlier this evening Doctor Wells said that he had *bolted* it, when he had left it *open*—purposely, as I now realize, in order that he might return later. You may also recall that Doctor Wells took a scrap of paper from Richard Fleming's hand and tried to conceal it. Why did he do *that?*"

She paused for a second. Then she changed her tone a little.

"May I ask you to look at this?"

She displayed the piece of paper on which Doctor Wells had started to write the prescription for her sleeping-powders—and now her strategy with the doctor's bag and the soot Jack Bailey had got from the fireplace stood revealed. A sharp, black imprint of a man's right thumb, the doctor's, stood out on the paper below the broken line of writing. The doctor had not noticed the staining of his hand by the blackened bag handle, or, noticing, had thought nothing of it. But the blackened bag handle had been a trap and he had left an indelible piece of evidence behind him. It now remained to test the value of this evidence.

Miss Cornelia handed the paper to Anderson silently. But her eyes were bright with pardonable vanity at the success of her little piece of strategy.

"A thumbprint," muttered Anderson. "Whose is it?"

"Doctor Wells," said Miss Cornelia with what might have been a little crow of triumph in anyone not a Van Gorder.

Anderson looked thoughtful. Then he felt in his pocket for a magnifying glass, failed to find it, muttered, and took the reading glass Miss Cornelia offered him.

"Try this," she said. "My whole case hangs on my conviction that that print and the one out there on the stair rail are the same."

He put down the paper and smiled at her ironically.

"Your case!" he said. "You don't really believe you need a detective at all, do you?"

"I will only say that so far your views and mine have failed to coincide. If I am right about that fingerprint, then you may be right about my private opinion."

And on that he went out, rather grimly, paper and reading glass in hand, to make his comparison.

It was then that Beresford came in, a new and slightly rigid Beresford, and crossed to her at once.

"Miss Van Gorder," he said, all the flippancy gone from his voice, "may I ask you to make an excuse and call your gardener here?"

Dale started uncontrollably at the ominous words, but Miss Cornelia betrayed no emotion except in the increased rapidity of her knitting.

"The gardener? Certainly, if you'll touch that bell," she said pleasantly.

Beresford stalked to the bell and rang it. The three waited—Dale in an agony of suspense.

The detective re-entered the room by the alcove

stairs, his mien unfathomable by any of the anxious glances that sought him out at once.

"It's no good, Miss Van Gorder," he said quietly. "The prints are not the same."

"Not the same!" gasped Miss Cornelia, unwilling to believe her ears.

Anderson laid down the paper and the reading glass with a little gesture of dismissal.

"If you think I'm mistaken, I'll leave it to any unprejudiced person or your own eyesight. Thumbprints never lie," he said in a flat, convincing voice. Miss Cornelia stared at him, disappointment written large on her features. He allowed himself a little ironic smile.

"Did you ever try a good cigar when you wanted to think?" he queried suavely, puffing upon his own.

But Miss Cornelia's spirit was too broken by the collapse of her dearly loved and adroitly managed scheme for her to take up the gauge of battle he offered.

"I still believe it was the doctor," she said stubbornly. But her tones were not the tones of utter conviction which she had used before.

"And yet," said the detective, ruthlessly demolishing another link in her broken chain of evidence, "the doctor was in this room tonight, according to your own statement, when the anonymous letter came through the window."

Miss Cornelia gazed at him blankly, for the first

time in her life at a loss for an appropriately sharp retort. It was true. The doctor had been here in the room beside her when the stone bearing the last anonymous warning had crashed through the window-pane. And yet—

Billy's entrance in answer to Beresford's ring made her mind turn to other matters for the moment. Why had Beresford's manner changed so, and what was he saying to Billy now?

"Tell the gardener Miss Van Gorder wants him and don't say we're all here," the young lawyer commanded the butler sharply. Billy nodded and disappeared. Miss Cornelia's back began to stiffen; she didn't like other people ordering her servants around like that.

The detective, apparently, had somewhat of the same feeling.

"I seem to have plenty of *help* in this case!" he said with obvious sarcasm, turning to Beresford.

The latter made no reply. Dale rose anxiously from her chair, her lips quivering.

"Why have you sent for the gardener?" she inquired haltingly.

Beresford deigned to answer at last.

"I'll tell you that in a moment," he said with a grim tightening of his lips.

There was a fateful pause, for an instant, while Dale roved nervously from one side of the room to the other. Then Jack Bailey came into the room—alone.

He seemed to sense danger in the air. His hands clenched at his sides, but except for that tiny betrayal of emotion, he still kept his servant's pose.

"You sent for me?" he queried Miss Cornelia submissively, ignoring the glowering Beresford.

But Beresford would be ignored no longer. He came between them before Miss Cornelia had time to answer.

"How long has this man been in your employ?" he asked brusquely, manner tense.

Miss Cornelia made one final attempt at evasion.

"Why should that interest you?" she parried, answering his question with an icy question of her own.

It was too late. Already Bailey had read the truth in Beresford's eyes.

"I came this evening," he admitted, still hoping against hope that his cringing posture of the servitor might give Beresford pause for the moment.

But the promptness of his answer only crystallized Beresford's suspicions.

"Exactly," he said with terse finality. He turned to the detective.

"I've been trying to recall this man's face ever since I came in tonight—" he said with grim triumph. "Now, I know who he is."

"Who is he?"

Bailey straightened up. He had lost his game with Chance. And the loss, coming when it did, seemed bitterer than even he had thought it could be, but before they took him away he would speak his mind.

"It's all right, Beresford," he said with a fatigue so deep that it colored his voice like flakes of iron-rust. "I know you think you're doing your duty but I wish to God you could have *restrained* your sense of duty for about three hours more!"

"To let you get away?" the young lawyer sneered, unconvinced.

"No," said Bailey with quiet defiance. "To let me finish what I came here to do."

"Don't you think you have done enough?" Beresford's voice flicked him with righteous scorn, no less telling because of its youthfulness. He turned back to the detective soberly enough.

"This man has imposed upon the credulity of these women, I am quite sure without their knowledge," he said with a trace of his former gallantry. "He is Bailey of the Union Bank, the missing cashier."

The detective slowly put down his cigar on an ash tray.

"That's the truth, is it?" he demanded.

Dale's hand flew to her breast. If Jack would only deny it — even now! But even as she thought this, she realized the uselessness of any such denial.

Bailey realized it, too.

"It's true, all right," he admitted hopelessly. He closed his eyes for a moment. Let them come with the handcuffs now and get it over. Every moment the scene dragged out was a moment of unnecessary torture for Dale.

But Beresford had not finished with his indictment.

"I accuse him not only of the thing he is wanted for, but of the murder of Richard Fleming!" he said fiercely, glaring at Bailey as if only a youthful horror of making a scene before Dale and Miss Cornelia held him back from striking the latter down where he stood.

Bailey's eyes snapped open. He took a threatening step toward his accuser. "You lie!" he said in a hoarse, violent voice.

Anderson crossed between them, just as conflict seemed inevitable.

"*You* knew this?" he queried sharply in Dale's direction.

Dale set her lips in a line. She did not answer.

He turned to Miss Cornelia.

"Did you?"

"Yes," admitted the latter quietly, her knitting needles at last at rest. "I knew he was Mr. Bailey if that is all you mean."

The quietness of her answer seemed to infuriate the detective.

"Quite a pretty little conspiracy," he said. "How in the name of God do you expect me to do anything with the entire household united against me? Tell me that."

"Exactly," said Miss Cornelia. "And if we are

united against you, why should I have sent for you? You might tell me that, too."

He turned on Bailey savagely.

"What did you mean by that 'three hours more'?" he demanded.

"I could have cleared myself in three hours," said Bailey with calm despair.

Beresford laughed mockingly—a laugh that seemed to sear into Bailey's consciousness like the touch of a hot iron. Again he turned frenziedly upon the young lawyer and Anderson was just preparing to hold them away from each other, by force if necessary, when the doorbell rang.

For an instant the ringing of the bell held the various figures of the little scene in the rigid postures of a waxworks tableau—Bailey, one foot advanced toward Beresford, his hand balled up into fists—Beresford already in an attitude of defense—the detective about to step in between them—Miss Cornelia stiff in her chair—Dale over by the fireplace, her hand at her heart. Then they relaxed, but not, at least on the part of Bailey and Beresford, to resume their interrupted conflict. Too many nerve-shaking things had already happened that night for either of the young men not to drop their mutual squabble in the face of a common danger.

"Probably the doctor," murmured Miss Cornelia uncertainly as the doorbell rang again. "He was to come back with some sleeping-powders."

Billy appeared for the key of the front door.

"If that's Doctor Wells," warned the detective, "admit him. If it's anybody else, call me."

Billy grinned acquiescently and departed. The detective moved nearer to Bailey.

"Have you got a gun on you?"

"No." Bailey bowed his head.

"Well, I'll just make sure of that." The detective's hands ran swiftly and expertly over Bailey's form, through his pockets, probing for concealed weapons. Then, slowly drawing a pair of handcuffs from his pocket, he prepared to put them on Bailey's wrists.

Chapter Fifteen: The Sign of the Bat

But Dale could bear it no longer. The sight of her lover, beaten, submissive, his head bowed, waiting obediently like a common criminal for the detective to lock his wrists in steel broke down her last defenses. She rushed into the center of the room, between Bailey and the detective, her eyes wild with terror, her words stumbling over each other in her eagerness to get them out.

"Oh, no! I can't stand it! I'll tell you everything!" she cried frenziedly. "He got to the foot of the staircase—Richard Fleming, I mean," she was facing the detective now, "and he had the blueprint you've been talking about. I had told him Jack Bailey was here as the gardener and he said if I screamed he would tell that. I was desperate. I threatened him with the revolver but he took it from me. Then when I tore the blueprint from him—he was shot—from the stairs—"

"By Bailey!" interjected Beresford angrily.

"I didn't even know he was in the house!" Bailey's

answer was as instant as it was hot. Meanwhile, the doctor had entered the room, hardly noticed, in the middle of Dale's confession, and now stood watching the scene intently from a post by the door.

"What did you do with the blueprint?" The detective's voice beat at Dale like a whip.

"I put it first in the neck of my dress—" she faltered. "Then, when I found you were watching me, I hid it somewhere else."

Her eyes fell on the doctor. She saw his hand steal out toward the knob of the door. Was he going to run away on some pretext before she could finish her story? She gave a sigh of relief when Billy, reentering with the key to the front door, blocked any such attempt at escape.

Mechanically she watched Billy cross to the table, lay the key upon it, and return to the hall without so much as a glance at the tense, suspicious circle of faces focused upon herself and her lover.

"I put it—somewhere else," she repeated, her eyes going back to the doctor.

"Did you give it to Bailey?"

"No—I hid it—and then I told where it was—to the doctor—" Dale swayed on her feet. All turned surprisedly toward the doctor. Miss Cornelia rose from her chair.

The doctor bore the battery of eyes unflinchingly.

"That's rather inaccurate," he said, with a tight little smile. "You told me where you had placed it, but when I went to look for it, it was gone."

"Are you quite sure of that?" queried Miss Cornelia acidly.

"Absolutely," he said. He ignored the rest of the party, addressing himself directly to Anderson.

"She said she had hidden it inside one of the rolls that were on the tray on that table," he continued in tones of easy explanation, approaching the table as he did so, and tapping it with the box of sleeping-powders he had brought for Miss Cornelia.

"She was in such distress that I finally went to look for it. It wasn't there."

"Do you realize the significance of this paper?" Anderson boomed at once.

"Nothing, beyond the fact that Miss Ogden was afraid it linked her with the crime." The doctor's voice was very clear and firm.

Anderson pondered an instant. Then—

"I'd like to have a few minutes with the doctor alone," he said somberly.

The group about him dissolved at once. Miss Cornelia, her arm around her niece's waist, led the latter gently to the door. As the two lovers passed each other a glance flashed between them—a glance, pathetically brief, of longing and love. Dale's finger tips brushed Bailey's hand gently in passing.

"Beresford," commanded the detective, "take Bailey to the library and see that he stays there."

Beresford tapped his pocket with a significant gesture and motioned Bailey to the door. Then they, too, left the room. The door closed. The doctor and the detective were alone.

The detective spoke at once—and surprisingly.

"Doctor, I'll have that blueprint!" he said sternly, his eyes the color of steel.

The doctor gave him a wary little glance.

"But I've just made the statement that I didn't find the blueprint," he affirmed flatly.

"I heard you!" Anderson's voice was very dry. "Now this situation is between you and me, Doctor Wells." His forefinger sought the doctor's chest. "It has nothing to do with that poor fool of a cashier. He hasn't got either those securities or the money from them and you know it. It's in this house and you know that, too!"

"In this house?" repeated the doctor as if stalling for time.

"In this house! Tonight, when you claimed to be making a professional call, you were in this house and I think you were on that staircase when Richard Fleming was killed!"

"No, Anderson, I'll swear I was not!" The doctor might be acting, but if he was, it was incomparable acting. The terror in his voice seemed too real to be feigned.

But Anderson was remorseless.

"I'll tell you this," he continued. "Miss Van Gorder very cleverly got a thumbprint of yours tonight. Does that mean anything to you?"

His eyes bored into the doctor, the eyes of a

213

poker player bluffing on a hidden card. But the doctor did not flinch.

"Nothing," he said firmly. "I have not been upstairs in this house in three months."

The accent of truth in his voice seemed so unmistakable that even Anderson's shrewd brain was puzzled by it. But he persisted in his attempt to wring a confession from this latest suspect.

"Before Courtleigh Fleming died — did he tell you anything about a Hidden Room in this house?" he queried cannily.

The doctor's confident air of honesty lessened, a furtive look appeared in his eyes.

"No," he insisted, but not as convincingly as he had made his previous denial.

The detective hammered at the point again.

"You haven't been trying to frighten these women out of here with anonymous letters so you could get in?"

"No. Certainly not." But again the doctor's air had that odd mixture of truth and falsehood in it.

The detective paused for an instant.

"Let me see your key ring!" he ordered. The doctor passed it over silently The detective glanced at the keys — then, suddenly, his revolver glittered in his other hand.

The doctor watched him anxiously. A puff of wind rattled the panes of the French windows. The storm, quieted for a while, was gathering its strength for a fresh unleashing of its dogs of thunder.

The detective stepped to the terrace door, opened it, and then quietly proceeded to try the doctor's keys in the lock. Thus located he was out of visual range, and Wells took advantage of it at once. He moved swiftly toward the fireplace, extracting the missing piece of blueprint from an inside pocket as he did so. The secret the blueprint guarded was already graven on his mind in indelible characters. Now he would destroy all evidence that it had ever been in his possession and bluff through the rest of the situation as best he might.

He threw the paper toward the flames with a nervous gesture of relief. But for once his cunning failed; the throw was too hurried to be sure and the light scrap of paper wavered and settled to the floor just outside the fireplace. The doctor swore noiselessly and stooped to pick it up and make sure of its destruction. But he was not quick enough. Through the window the detective had seen the incident, and the next moment the doctor heard his voice bark behind him. He turned, and stared at the leveled muzzle of Anderson's revolver.

"Hands up and stand back!" he commanded.

As he did so Anderson picked up the paper and a sardonic smile crossed his face as his eyes took in the significance of the print. He laid his revolver down on the table where he could snatch it up again at a moment's notice.

"Behind a fireplace, eh?" he muttered. "What

fireplace? In what room?"

"I won't tell you!" The doctor's voice was sullen. He inched, gingerly, cautiously, toward the other side of the table.

"All right — I'll find it, you know." The detective's eyes turned swiftly back to the blueprint. Experience should have taught him never to underrate an adversary, even of the doctor's caliber, but long familiarity with danger can make the shrewdest careless. For a moment, as he bent over the paper again, he was off guard.

The doctor seized the moment with a savage promptitude and sprang. There followed a silent, furious struggle between the two. Under normal circumstances Anderson would have been the stronger and quicker, but the doctor fought with an added strength of despair and his initial leap had pinioned the detective's arms behind him. Now the detective shook one hand free and snatched at the revolver — in vain — for the doctor, with a groan of desperation, struck at his hand as its fingers were about to close on the smooth butt and the revolver skidded from the table to the floor. With a sudden terrible movement he pinioned both the detective's arms behind him again and reached for the telephone. Its heavy base descended on the back of the detective's head with stunning force. The next moment the battle was ended and the doctor, panting with exhaustion, held the limp form of an unconscious man in his arms.

He lowered the detective to the floor and straightened up again, listening tensely. So brief and intense had been the struggle that even now he could hardly believe in its reality. It seemed impossible, too, that the struggle had not been heard. Then he realized dully, as a louder roll of thunder smote on his ears, that the elements themselves had played into his hand. The storm, with its wind and fury, had returned just in time to save him and drown out all sounds of conflict from the rest of the house with its giant clamor.

He bent swiftly over Anderson, listening to his heart. Good—the man still breathed; he had enough on his conscience without adding the murder of a detective to the black weight. Now he pocketed the revolver and the blueprint, gagged Anderson rapidly with a knotted handkerchief and proceeded to wrap his own muffler around the detective's head as an additional silencer. Anderson gave a faint sigh.

The doctor thought rapidly. Soon or late the detective would return to consciousness; with his hands free he could easily tear out the gag. He looked wildly around the room for a rope, a curtain—ah, he had it—the detective's own handcuffs! He snapped the cuffs on Anderson's wrists, then realized that, in his hurry, he had bound the detective's hands in front of him instead of behind him. Well, it would do for the moment; he did not need much time to carry out his plans. He dragged the limp body, its head lolling, into the billiard room where he deposited it on the floor in the corner farthest from the door.

So far, so good. Now to lock the door of the billiard room. Fortunately, the key was there on the inside of the door. He quickly transferred it, locked the billiard-room door from the outside, and pocketed the key. For a second he stood by the center table in the living-room, recovering his breath and trying to straighten his rumpled clothing. Then he crossed cautiously into the alcove and started to pad up the alcove stairs, his face white and strained with excitement and hope.

And it was then that there happened one of the most dramatic events of the night. One which was to remain, for the next hour or so, as bewildering as the murder and which, had it come a few moments sooner or a few moments later, would have entirely changed the course of events.

It was preceded by a desperate hammering on the door of the terrace. It halted the doctor on his way upstairs, drew Beresford on a run into the living-room, and even reached the bedrooms of the women up above.

"My God! What's that?" Beresford panted.

The doctor indicated the door. It was too late now. Already he could hear Miss Cornelia's voice above; it was only a question of a short time until Anderson in the billiard room revived and would try to make his plight known. And in the brief moment of that résumé of his position the knocking came again. But feebler, as though the suppliant outside had exhausted his strength.

As Beresford drew his revolver and moved to the door, Miss Cornelia came in, followed by Lizzie.

"It's the Bat," Lizzie announced mournfully. "Good-by, Miss Neily. Good-by, everybody. I saw his hand, all covered with blood. He's had a good night for sure!"

But they ignored her. And Beresford flung open the door.

Just what they had expected, what figure of horror or of fear they waited for, no one can say. But there was no horror and no fear; only unutterable amazement as an unknown man, in torn and muddied garments, with a streak of dried blood seaming his forehead like a scar, fell through the open doorway into Beresford's arms.

"Good God!" muttered Beresford, dropping his revolver to catch the strange burden. For a moment the Unknown lay in his arms like a corpse. Then he straighted dizzily, staggered into the room, took a few steps toward the table, and fell prostrate upon his face—at the end of his strength.

"Doctor!" gasped Miss Cornelia dazedly and the doctor, whatever guilt lay on his conscience, responded at once to the call of his profession.

He bent over the Unknown Man—the physician once more—and made a brief examination.

"He's fainted!" he said, rising. "Struck on the

219

head, too."

"But *who is he?*" faltered Miss Cornelia.

"I never saw him before," said the doctor. It was obvious that he spoke the truth. "Does anyone recognize him?"

All crowded about the Unknown, trying to read the riddle of his identity. Miss Cornelia rapidly revised her first impressions of the stranger. When he had first fallen through the doorway into Beresford's arms she had not known what to think. Now, in the brighter light of the living-room she saw that the still face, beneath its mask of dirt and dried blood, was strong and fairly youthful; if the man were a criminal, he belonged, like the Bat, to the upper fringes of the world of crime. She noted mechanically that his hands and feet had been tied, ends of frayed rope still dangled from his wrists and ankles. And that terrible injury on his head! She shuddered and closed her eyes.

"Does anyone recognize him?" repeated the doctor but one by one the others shook their heads. Crook, casual tramp, or honest laborer unexpectedly caught in the sinister toils of the Cedarcrest affair — his identity seemed a mystery to one and all.

"Is he badly hurt?" asked Miss Cornelia, shuddering again.

"It's hard to say," answered the doctor. "I think not."

The Unknown stirred feebly, made an effort to sit

up. Beresford and the doctor caught him under the arms and helped him to his feet. He stood there swaying, a blank expression on his face.

"A chair!" said the doctor quickly. "Ah—" He helped the strange figure to sit down and bent over him again.

"You're all right now, my friend," he said in his best tones of professional cheeriness. "Dizzy a bit, aren't you?"

The Unknown rubbed his wrists where his bonds had cut them. He made an effort to speak.

"Water!" he said in a low voice.

The doctor gestured to Billy. "Get some water— or whisky—if there is any—that'd be better."

"There's a flask of whisky in my room, Billy," added Miss Cornelia helpfully.

"Now, my man," continued the doctor to the Unknown. "You're in the hands of friends. Brace up and tell us what happened!"

Beresford had been looking about for the detective, puzzled not to find him, as usual, in charge of affairs. Now, "Where's Anderson? This is a police matter!" he said, making a movement as if to go in search of him.

The doctor stopped him quickly.

"He was here a minute ago, he'll be back presently," he said, praying to whatever gods he served that Anderson, bound and gagged in the billiard room, had not yet returned to consciousness.

Unobserved by all except Miss Cornelia, the men-

221

tion of the detective's name had caused a strange reaction in the Unknown. His eyes had opened—he had started—the haze in his mind had seemed to clear away for a moment. Then, for some reason, his shoulders had slumped again and the look of apathy come back to his face. But, stunned or not, it now seemed possible that he was not quite as dazed as he appeared.

The doctor gave the slumped shoulders a little shake.

"Rouse yourself, man!" he said. "What has happened to you?"

"I'm dazed!" said the Unknown thickly and slowly. "I can't remember." He passed a hand weakly over his forehead.

"What a night!" sighed Miss Cornelia, sinking into a chair. "Richard Fleming murdered in this house—and now—this!"

The Unknown shot her a stealthy glance from beneath lowered eyelids. But when she looked at him, his face was blank again.

"Why doesn't somebody ask his name?" queried Dale, and "Where the devil is that detective?" muttered Beresford, almost in the same instant.

Neither question was answered, and Beresford, increasingly uneasy at the continued absence of Anderson, turned toward the hall.

The doctor took Dale's suggestion.

"What's your name?"

Silence from the Unknown—and that blank stare

of stupefaction.

"Look at his papers." It was Miss Cornelia's voice. The doctor and Bailey searched the torn trouser pockets, the pockets of the muddied shirt, while the Unknown submitted passively, not seeming to care what happened to him. But search him as they would—it was in vain.

"Not a paper on him," said Jack Bailey at last, straightening up.

A crash of breaking glass from the head of the alcove stairs put a period to his sentence. All turned toward the stairs—or all except the Unknown, who, for a moment, half-rose in his chair, his eyes gleaming, his face alert, the mask of bewildered apathy gone from his face.

As they watched, a rigid little figure of horror backed slowly down the alcove stairs and into the room—Billy, the Japanese, his Oriental placidity disturbed at last, incomprehensible terror written in every line of his face.

"Billy!"

"Billy, what is it?"

The diminutive butler made a pitiful attempt at his usual grin.

"It—nothing," he gasped. The Unknown relapsed in his chair—again the dazed stranger from nowhere.

Beresford took the Japanese by the shoulders.

"Now see here!" he said sharply. "You've seen something! What was it!"

223

Billy trembled like a leaf.

"Ghost! Ghost!" he muttered frantically, his face working.

"He's concealing something. Look at him!" Miss Cornelia stared at her servant.

"No, no!" insisted Billy in an ague of fright. "No, no!"

But Miss Cornelia was sure of it.

"Brooks, close that door!" she said, pointing at the terrace door in the alcove which still stood ajar after the entrance of the Unknown.

Bailey moved to obey. But just as he reached the alcove the terrace door slammed shut in his face. At the same moment every light in Cedarcrest blinked and went out again.

Bailey fumbled for the doorknob in the sudden darkness.

"The door's *locked!*" he said incredulously. "The key's gone too. Where's your revolver, Beresford?"

"I dropped it in the alcove when I caught that man," called Beresford, cursing himself for his carelessness.

The illuminated dial of Bailey's wrist watch flickered in the darkness as he searched for the revolver—a round, glowing spot of phosphorescence.

Lizzie screamed. "The eye! The gleaming eye I saw on the stairs!" she shrieked, pointing at it frenziedly.

"Quick—there's a candle on the table—light it somebody. Never mind the revolver, I have one!"

224

called Miss Cornelia.

"Righto!" called Beresford in reply. He found the candle, lit it —

The group blinked at each other for a moment, still unable to co-ordinate their thoughts.

Bailey ratted the knob of the door into the hall.

"This door's locked, too!" he said with increasing puzzlement. A gasp went over the group. They were locked in the room while some devilment was going on in the rest of the house. That they knew. But what it might be, what form it might take, they had not the remotest idea. They were too distracted to notice the injured man, now alert in his chair, or the doctor's odd attitude of listening, above the rattle and banging of the storm.

But it was not until Miss Cornelia took the candle and proceeded toward the hall door to examine it that the full horror of the situation burst upon them.

Neatly fastened to the white panel of the door, chest high and hardly more than just dead, was the body of a bat.

Of what happened thereafter no one afterward remembered the details. To be shut in there at the mercy of one who knew no mercy was intolerable. It was left for Miss Cornelia to remember her own revolver, lying unnoticed on the table since the crime earlier in the evening, and to suggest its use in shattering the lock.

Just what they had expected when the door was

finally opened they did not know. But the house was quiet and in order; no new horror faced them in the hall; their candle revealed no bloody figure, their ears heard no unearthly sound.

Slowly they began to breathe normally once more.

After that they began to search the house. Since no room was apparently immune from danger, the men made no protest when the women insisted on accompanying them. And as time went on and chamber after chamber was discovered empty and undisturbed, gradually the courage of the party began to rise. Lizzie, still whimpering, stuck closely to Miss Cornelia's heels, but that spirited lady began to make small side excursions of her own.

Of the men, only Bailey, Beresford, and the doctor could really be said to search at all. Billy had remained below, impassive of face but rolling of eye; the Unknown, after an attempt to depart with them, had sunk back weakly into his chair again, and the detective, Anderson, was still unaccountably missing.

While no one could be said to be grieving over this, still the belief that somehow, somewhere, he had met the Bat and suffered at his hands was strong in all of them except the doctor. As each door was opened they expected to find him, probably foully murdered; as each door was closed again they breathed with relief.

And as time went on and the silence and peace

remained unbroken, the conviction grew on them that the Bat had in this manner achieved his object and departed; had done his work, signed it after his usual fashion, and gone.

And thus were matters when Miss Cornelia, happening on the attic staircase with Lizzie at her heels, decided to look about her up there. And went up.

Chapter Sixteen: The Hidden Room

A few moments later Jack Bailey, seeing a thin glow of candlelight from the attic above and hearing Lizzie's protesting voice, made his way up there. He found them in the trunk room, a dusty, dingy apartment lined with high closets along the walls—the floor littered with an incongruous assortment of attic objects—two battered trunks, a clothes hamper, an old sewing machine, a broken-backed kitchen chair, two dilapidated suitcases and a shabby satchel that might once have been a woman's dressing case—in one corner a grimy fireplace in which, obviously, no fire had been lighted for years.

But he also found Miss Cornelia holding her candle to the floor and staring at something there.

"Candle grease!" she said sharply, staring at a line of white spots by the window. She stooped and touched the spots with an exploratory finger.

"Fresh candle grease! Now who do you suppose did that? Do you remember how Mr. Gillette, in

Sherlock Holmes, when he—"

Her voice trailed off. She stooped and followed the trail of the candle grease away from the window, ingeniously trying to copy the shrewd, piercing gaze of Mr. Gillette as she remembered him in his most famous role.

"It leads straight to the fireplace!" she murmured in tones of Sherlockian gravity. Bailey repressed an involuntary smile. But her next words gave him genuine food for thought.

She stared at the mantel of the fireplace accusingly.

"It's been going through my mind for the last few minutes that no chimney flue runs up this side of the house!" she said.

Bailey stared. "Then why the fireplace?"

"That's what I'm going to find out!" said the spinster grimly. She started to rap the mantel, testing it for secret springs.

"Jack! Jack!" It was Dale's voice, low and cautious, coming from the landing of the stairs.

Bailey stepped to the door of the trunk room.

"Come in," he called in reply. "And shut the door behind you."

Dale entered, closing the door behind her.

"Where are the others?"

"They're still searching the house. There's no sign of anybody."

"They haven't found—Mr. Anderson?"

Dale shook her head. "Not yet."

229

She turned toward her aunt. Miss Cornelia had begun to enjoy herself once more.

Rapping on the mantelpiece, poking and pressing various corners and sections of the mantel itself, she remembered all the detective stories she had ever read and thought, with a sniff of scorn, that she could better them. There were always sliding panels and hidden drawers in detective stories and the detective discovered them by rapping just as she was doing, and listening for a hollow sound in answer. She rapped on the wall above the mantel — exactly — there was the hollow echo she wanted.

"Hollow as Lizzie's head!" she said triumphantly. The fireplace was obviously not what it seemed, there must be a space behind it unaccounted for in the building plans. Now what was the next step detectives always took? Oh, yes — they looked for panels; panels that moved. And when one shoved them away there was a button or something. She pushed and pressed and finally something did move. It was the mantelpiece itself, false grate and all, which begin to swing out into the room, revealing behind a dark, hollow cubbyhole, some six feet by six — the Hidden Room at last!

"Oh, Jack, be careful!" breathed Dale as her lover took Miss Cornelia's candle and moved toward the dark hiding-place. But her eyes had already caught the outlines of a tall iron safe in the gloom and in spite of her fears, her lips formed a wordless cry of victory.

But Jack Bailey said nothing at all. One glance had shown him that the safe was empty.

The tragic collapse of all their hopes was almost more than they could bear. Coming on top of the nerve-racking events of the night, it left them dazed and directionless. It was, of course, Miss Cornelia who recovered first.

"Even without the money," she said, "the mere presence of this safe here, hidden away, tells the story. The fact that someone else knew and got here first cannot alter that."

But she could not cheer them. It was Lizzie who created a diversion. Lizzie who had bolted into the hall at the first motion of the mantelpiece outward and who now, with equal precipitation, came bolting back. She rushed into the room, slamming the door behind her, and collapsed into a heap of moaning terror at her mistress's feet. At first she was completely inarticulate, but after a time she muttered that she had seen "him" and then fell to groaning again.

The same thought was in all their minds, that in some corner of the upper floor she had come across the body of Anderson. But when Miss Cornelia finally quieted her and asked this, she shook her head.

"It was the Bat I saw," was her astounding statement. "He dropped through the skylight out there and ran along the hall. I *saw* him I tell you. He went right by me!"

231

"Nonsense," said Miss Cornelia briskly. "How can you say such a thing?"

But Bailey pushed forward and took Lizzie by the shoulder.

"What did he look like?"

"He hadn't any face. He was all black where his face ought to be."

"Do you mean he wore a mask?"

"Maybe. I don't know."

She collapsed again but when Bailey, followed by Miss Cornelia, made a move toward the door she broke into frantic wailing.

"Don't go out there!" she shrieked. "He's there I tell you. I'm not crazy. If you open that door, he'll shoot."

But the door was already open and no shot came. With the departure of Bailey and Miss Cornelia, and the resulting darkness due to their taking the candle, Lizzie and Dale were left alone. The girl was faint with disappointment and strain; she sat huddled on a trunk, saying nothing, and after a moment or so Lizzie roused to her condition.

"Not feeling sick, are you?" she asked.

"I feel a little queer."

"Who wouldn't in the dark here with that monster loose somewhere near by?" But she stirred herself and got up. "I'd better get the smelling salts," she said heavily. "God knows I hate to move, but if there's one place safer in this house than another, I've yet to find it."

She went out, leaving Dale alone. The trunk room was dark, save that now and then as the candle appeared and reappeared the doorway was faintly outlined. On this outline she kept her eyes fixed, by way of comfort, and thus passed the next few moments. She felt weak and dizzy and entirely despairing.

Then—the outline was not so clear. She had heard nothing but there was something in the doorway. It stood there, formless, diabolical, and then she saw what was happening. It was closing the door. Afterward she was mercifully not to remember what came next; the figure was perhaps intent on what was going on outside, or her own movements may have been as silent as its own. That she got into the mantel-room and even partially closed it behind her is certain, and that her description of what followed is fairly accurate is borne out by the facts as known.

The Bat was working rapidly. She heard his quick, nervous movements; apparently he had come back for something and secured it, for now he moved again toward the door. But he was too late; they were returning that way. She heard him mutter something and quickly turn the key in the lock. Then he seemed to run toward the window, and for some reason to recoil from it.

The next instant she realized that he was coming toward the mantel-room, that he intended to hide in it. There was no doubt in her mind as to his iden-

233

tity. It was the Bat, and in a moment more he would be shut in there with her.

She tried to scream and could not, and the next instant, when the Bat leaped into concealment beside her, she was in a dead faint on the floor.

Bailey meanwhile had crawled out on the roof and was carefully searching it. But other things were happening also. A disinterested observer could have seen very soon why the Bat had abandoned the window as a means of egress.

Almost before the mantel had swung to behind the archcriminal, the top of a tall pruning ladder had appeared at the window and by its quivering showed that someone was climbing up, rung by rung. Unsuspiciously enough he came on, pausing at the top to flash a light into the room, and then cautiously swinging a leg over the sill. It was the doctor. He gave a low whistle but there was no reply, save that, had he seen it, the mantel swung out an inch or two. Perhaps he was never so near death as that movement but that instant of irresolution on his part saved him, for by coming into the room he had taken himself out of range.

Even then he was very close to destruction, for after a brief pause and a second rather puzzled survey of the room, he started toward the mantel itself. Only the rattle of the doorknob stopped him, and a call from outside.

"Dale!" called Bailey's voice from the corridor. "Dale!"

"Dale! Dale! The door's locked!" cried Miss Cornelia.

The doctor hesitated. The call came again.

"Dale! Dale!" and Bailey pounded on the door as if he meant to break it down.

The doctor made up his mind.

"Wait a moment!" he called. He stepped to the door and unlocked it. Bailey hurled himself into the room, followed by Miss Cornelia with her candle. Lizzie stood in the doorway, timidly, ready to leap for safety at a moment's notice.

"Why did you lock that door?" said Bailey angrily, threatening the doctor.

"But I didn't," said the latter, truthfully enough. Bailey made a movement of irritation. Then a glance about the room informed him of the amazing, the incredible fact. Dale was not there! She had disappeared!

"You—you," he stammered at the doctor. "Where's Miss Ogden? What have you done with her?"

The doctor was equally baffled.

"Done with her?" he said indignantly. "I don't know what you're talking about, I haven't seen her!"

"Then you didn't lock that door?" Bailey menaced him.

The doctor's denial was firm.

"Absolutely not. I was coming through the window when I heard your voice at the door!"

Bailey's eyes leaped to the window—yes—a ladder was there. The doctor might be speaking the truth after all. But if so, how and why had Dale disappeared?

The doctor's admission of his manner of entrance did not make Lizzie any the happier.

"In at the window—just like a bat!" she muttered in shaking tones. She would not have stayed in the doorway if she had not been afraid to move anywhere else.

"I saw lights up here from outside," continued the doctor easily. "And I thought—"

Miss Cornelia interrupted him. She had set down her candle and laid the revolver on the top of the clothes hamper and now stood gazing at the mantel-fireplace.

"The mantel's—closed!" she said.

The doctor stared. So the secret of the Hidden Room was a secret no longer. He saw ruin gaping before him—a bottomless abyss. "Damnation!" he cursed impotently under his breath.

Bailey turned on him savagely.

"Did you shut that mantel?"

"No!"

"I'll see whether you shut it or not!" Bailey leaped toward the fireplace. "Dale! Dale!" he called desperately, leaning against the mantel. His fingers groped for the knob that worked the mechanism of the hidden entrance.

The doctor picked up the single lighted candle

236

from the hamper, as if to throw more light on Bailey's task. Bailey's fingers found the knob. He turned it. The mantel begin to swing out into the room.

As it did so the doctor deliberately snuffed out the light of the candle he held, leaving the room in abrupt and obliterating darkness.

Chapter Seventeen:
Anderson Makes An Arrest

"Doctor, why did you put out that candle?" Miss Cornelia's voice cut the blackness like a knife.

"I didn't — I —"

"You did. I saw you do it."

The brief exchange of accusation and denial took but an instant of time, as the mantel swung wide open. The next instant there was a rush of feet across the floor, from the fireplace — the shock of a collision between two bodies — the sound of a heavy fall.

"What was that?" queried Bailey dazedly, with a feeling as if some great winged creature had brushed at him and passed.

Lizzie answered from the doorway.

"Oh, oh!" she groaned in stricken accents. "Somebody knocked me down and tramped on me!"

"Matches, quick!" commanded Miss Cornelia. "Where's the candle?"

The doctor was still trying to explain his curious

action of a moment before.

"Awfully sorry, I assure you. It dropped out of the holder—ah, here it is!"

He held it up triumphantly. Bailey struck a match and lighted it. The wavering little flame showed Lizzie prostrate but vocal, in the doorway—and Dale lying on the floor of the Hidden Room, her eyes shut, and her face as drained of color as the face of a marble statue. For one horrible instant Bailey thought she must be dead.

He rushed to her wildly and picked her up in his arms. No—still breathing—thank God! He carried her tenderly to the only chair in the room.

"Doctor!"

The doctor, once more the physician, knelt at her side and felt for her pulse. And Lizzie, picking herself up from where the collision with some violent body had throw her, retrieved the smelling salts from the floor. It was onto this picture—the candlelight shining on strained faces, the dramatic figure of Dale, now semi-conscious, the desperate rage of Bailey—that a new actor appeared on the scene.

Anderson, the detective, stood in the doorway, holding a candle—as grim and menacing a figure as a man just arisen from the dead.

"That's right!" said Lizzie, unappalled for once. "Come in when everything's over!"

The doctor glanced up and met the detective's eyes, cold and menacing.

"You took my revolver from me downstairs," he said. "I'll trouble you for it."

239

The doctor got heavily to his feet. The others, their suspicions confirmed at last, looked at him with startled eyes. The detective seemed to enjoy the universal confusion his words had brought.

Slowly, with sullen reluctance, the doctor yielded up the stolen weapon. The detective examined it casually and replaced it in his hip pocket.

"I've something to settle with you pretty soon," he said through clenched teeth, addressing the doctor. "And I'll settle it properly. Now, what's this?"

He indicated Dale, her face still and waxen, her breath coming so faintly she seemed hardly to breathe at all as Miss Cornelia and Bailey tried to revive her.

"She's coming to—" said Miss Cornelia triumphantly, as a first faint flush of color reappeared in the girl's cheeks. "We found her shut in there, Mr. Anderson," the spinster added, pointing toward the gaping entrance of the Hidden Room.

A gleam crossed the detective's face. He went up to examine the secret chamber. As he did so, Doctor Wells, who had been inching surreptitiously toward the door, sought the opportunity of slipping out unobserved.

But Anderson was not to be caught napping again.

"Wells!" he barked. The doctor stopped and turned.

"Where were you when she was locked in this room?"

The doctor's eyes sought the floor—the walls—

wildly—for any possible loophole of escape.

"I didn't shut her in if that's what you mean!" he said defiantly. "There was *someone* shut in there with her!" He gestured at the Hidden Room. "Ask these people here."

Miss Cornelia caught him up at once.

"The fact remains, Doctor," she said, her voice cold with anger, "that we left her here alone. When we came back you were here. The corridor door was locked, and she was in that room—unconscious!"

She moved forward to throw the light of her candle on the Hidden Room as the detective passed into it, gave it a swift professional glance, and stepped out again. But she had not finished her story by any means.

"As we opened that door," she continued to the detective, tapping the false mantel, "the doctor deliberately extinguished our only candle!"

"Do you know who was in that room?" queried the detective fiercely, wheeling on the doctor.

But the latter had evidently made up his mind to cling stubbornly to a policy of complete denial.

"No," he said sullenly. "I didn't put out the candle. It fell. And I didn't lock that door into the hall. I found it locked!"

A sigh of relief from Bailey now centered everyone's attention on himself and Dale. At last the girl was recovering from the shock of her terrible experience and regaining consciousness. Her eyelids fluttered, closed again, opened once more. She tried to sit up, weakly, clinging to Bailey's shoulder. The color returned to her cheeks, the stupor left her eyes.

She gave the Hidden Room a hunted little glance and then shuddered violently.

"Please close that awful door," she said in a tremulous voice. "I don't want to see it again."

The detective went silently to close the iron doors.

"What happened to you? Can't you remember?" faltered Bailey, on his knees at her side.

The shadow of an old terror lay on the girl's face.

"I was in here alone in the dark," she began slowly—"Then, as I looked at the doorway there, I saw there was somebody there. He came in and closed the door. I didn't know what to do, so I slipped in—there, and after a while I knew he was coming in too, for he couldn't get out. Then I must have fainted."

"There was nothing about the figure that you recognized?"

"No. Nothing."

"But we know it was the Bat," put in Miss Cornelia.

The detective laughed sardonically. The old duel of opposing theories between the two seemed about to recommence.

"Still harping on the Bat!" he said, with a little sneer.

Miss Cornelia stuck to her guns.

"I have every reason to believe that the Bat is in this house," she said.

The detective gave another jarring, mirthless laugh.

"And that he took the Union Bank, money out of the safe, I suppose?" he jeered. "No, Miss Van Gorder."

He wheeled on the doctor now.

"Ask the doctor who took the Union Bank money out of that safe!" he thundered. "Ask the doctor who attacked me downstairs in the living-room, knocked me senseless, and locked me in the billiard room!"

There was an astounded silence. The detective added a parting shot to his indictment of the doctor.

"The next time you put handcuffs on a man be sure to take the key out of his vest pocket," he said, biting off the words.

Rage and consternation mingled on the doctor's countenance; on the faces of the others astonishment was followed by a growing certainty. Only Miss Cornelia clung stubbornly to her original theory.

"Perhaps I'm an obstinate old woman," she said in tones which obviously showed that if so she was rather proud of it, "but the doctor and all the rest of us were locked in the living-room not ten minutes ago!"

"By the Bat, I suppose!" mocked Anderson.

"By the Bat!" insisted Miss Cornelia inflexibly. "Who else would have fastened a dead bat to the door downstairs? Who else would have the bravado

243

to do that? Or what you call the imagination?"

In spite of himself Anderson seemed to be impressed.

"The Bat, eh?" he muttered, then, changing his tone, "You knew about this hidden room, Wells?" he shot at the doctor.

"Yes." The doctor bowed his head.

"And you knew the money was in the room?"

"Well, I was wrong, wasn't I?" parried the doctor. "You can look for yourself. That safe is empty."

The detective brushed his evasive answer aside.

"You were up in this room earlier tonight," he said in tones of apparent certainty.

"No, I couldn't *get* up!" the doctor still insisted, with strange violence for a man who had already admitted such damning knowledge.

The detective's face was a study in disbelief.

"You know where that money is, Wells, and I'm going to find it!"

This last taunt seemed to goad the doctor beyond endurance.

"Good God!" he shouted recklessly. "Do you suppose if I knew where it is, I'd be here? I've had plenty of chances to get away! No, you can't pin anything on me, Anderson! It isn't criminal to have known that room is here."

He paused, trembling with anger and, curiously enough, with an anger that seemed at least half sincere.

"Oh, don't be so damned virtuous!" said the detective brutally. "Maybe you haven't been upstairs

244

but, unless I miss my guess, you know who was!"

The doctor's face changed a little.

"What about Richard Fleming?" persisted the detective scornfully.

The doctor drew himself up.

"I never killed him!" he said so impressively that even Bailey's faith in his guilt was shaken. "I don't even own a revolver!"

The detective alone maintained his attitude unchanged.

"You come with me, Wells," he ordered, with a jerk of his thumb toward the door. "This time I'll do the locking up."

The doctor, head bowed, prepared to obey. The detective took up a candle to light their path. Then he turned to the others for a moment.

"Better get the young lady to bed," he said with a gruff kindliness of manner. "I think that I can promise you a quiet night from now on."

"I'm glad you think so, Mr. Anderson!" Miss Cornelia insisted on the last word. The detective ignored the satiric twist of her speech, motioned the doctor out ahead of him, and followed. The faint glow of his candle flickered a moment and vanished toward the stairs.

It was Bailey who broke the silence.

"I can believe a good bit about Wells," he said, "but not that he stood on that staircase and killed Dick Fleming."

Miss Cornelia roused from deep thought.

"Of course not," she said briskly. "Go down and

fix Miss Dale's bed, Lizzie. And then bring up some wine."

"Down there, where the Bat is?" Lizzie demanded.

"The Bat has gone."

"Don't you believe it. He's just got his hand in!"

But at last Lizzie went, and, closing the door behind her, Miss Cornelia proceeded more or less to think out loud.

"Suppose," she said, "that the Bat, or whoever it was shut in there with you, killed Richard Fleming. Say that he is the one Lizzie saw coming in by the terrace door. Then he knew where the money was for he went directly up the stairs. But that is two hours ago or more. Why didn't he get the money, if it was here, and get away?"

"He may have had trouble with the combination."

"Perhaps. Anyhow, he was on the small staircase when Dick Fleming started up, and of course he shot him. That's clear enough. Then he finally got the safe open, after locking us in below, and my coming up interrupted him. How on earth did he get out on the roof?"

Bailey glanced out the window.

"It would be possible from here. Possible, but not easy."

"But, if he could do that," she persisted, "he could have got away, too. There are trellises and porches. Instead of that he came back here to this room." She stared at the window. "Could a man have done that with one hand?"

246

"Never in the world."

Saying nothing, but deeply thoughtful, Miss Cornelia made a fresh progress around the room.

"I know very little about bank-currency," she said finally. "Could such a sum as was looted from the Union Bank be carried away in a man's pocket?"

Bailey considered the question.

"Even in bills of large denomination it would make a pretty sizeable bundle," he said.

But that Miss Cornelia's deductions were correct, whatever they were, was in question when Lizzie returned with the elderberry wine. Apparently Miss Cornelia was to be like the man who repaired the clock: she still had certain things left over.

For Lizzie announced that the Unknown was ranging the second floor hall. From the time they had escaped from the living-room this man had not been seen or thought of, but that he was a part of the mystery there could by no doubt. It flashed over Miss Cornelia, that, although he could not possibly have locked them in, in the darkness that followed he could easily have fastened the bat to the door. For the first time it occurred to her that the arch-criminal might not be working alone, and that the entrance of the Unknown might have been a carefully devised ruse to draw them all together and hold them there.

Nor was Beresford's arrival with the statement that the Unknown was moving through the house below particularly comforting.

"He may be dazed, or he may not," he said. "Personally, this is not a time to trust anybody."

Beresford knew nothing of what had just occurred, and now seeing Bailey he favored him with an ugly glance.

"In the absence of Anderson, Bailey," he added, "I don't propose to trust you too far. I'm making it my business from now on to see that you don't try to get away. Get that?"

But Bailey heard him without particular resentment.

"All right," he said. "But I'll tell you this. Anderson is here and has arrested the doctor. Keep your eye on me, if you think it's your duty, but don't talk to me as if I were a criminal. You don't know that yet."

"The doctor!" Beresford gasped.

But Miss Cornelia's keen ears had heard a sound outside and her eyes were focused on the door.

"The doorknob is moving," she said in a hushed voice.

Beresford moved to the door and jerked it violently open.

The butler, Billy, almost pitched into the room.

Chapter Eighteen: The Bat Still Flies

He stepped back in the doorway, looked out, then turned to them again.

"I come in, please?" he said pathetically, his hands quivering. "I not like to stay in dark."

Miss Cornelia took pity on him.

"Come in, Billy, of course. What is it? Anything the matter?"

Billy glanced about nervously.

"Man with sore head."

"What about him?"

"Act very strange." Again Billy's slim hands trembled.

Beresford broke in. "The man who fell into the room downstairs?"

Billy nodded.

"Yes. On second floor, walking around."

Beresford smiled, a bit smugly.

"I told you!" he said to Miss Cornelia. "I didn't think he was as dazed as he pretended to be."

Miss Cornelia, too, had been pondering the problem of the Unknown. She reached a swift decision. If he were what he pretended to be, a dazed wanderer, he could do them no harm. If he were not, a little strategy properly employed might unravel the whole mystery.

"Bring him up here, Billy," she said, turning to the butler.

Billy started to obey. But the darkness of the corridor seemed to appall him anew the moment he took a step toward it.

"You give candle, please?" he asked with a pleading expression. "Don't like dark."

Miss Cornelia handed him one of the two precious candles. Then his present terror reminded her of that one other occasion when she had seen him lose completely his stoic Oriental calm.

"Billy," she queried, "what did you see when you came running down the stairs before we were locked in, down below?"

The candle shook like a reed in Billy's grasp.

"Nothing!" he gasped with obvious untruth, though it did not seem so much as if he wished to conceal what he had seen as that he was trying to convince himself he had seen nothing.

"Nothing!" said Lizzie scornfully. "It was some nothing that would make him drop a bottle of whiskey!"

But Billy only backed toward the door, smiling apologetically.

"Thought I saw ghost," he said, and went out and down the stairs, the candlelight flickering, growing fainter, and finally disappearing. Silence and eerie darkness enveloped them all as they waited. And suddenly out of the blackness came a sound.

Something was flapping and thumping around the room.

"That's damned odd," muttered Beresford uneasily. "There *is* something moving around the room."

"It's up near the ceiling!" cried Bailey as the sound began again.

Lizzie began a slow wail of doom and disaster. "Oh—h—h—h—"

"Good God!" cried Beresford abruptly. "It hit me in the face!" He slapped his hands together in a vain attempt to capture the flying intruder.

Lizzie rose.

"I'm going!" she announced. "I don't know where, but I'm going!"

She took a wild step in the direction of the door. Then the flapping noise was all about her, her nose was bumped by an invisible object and she gave a horrified shriek.

"It's in my hair!" she screamed madly. "It's in my hair!"

The next instant Baily gave a triumphant cry.

"I've got it! It's a bat!"

Lizzie sank to her knees, still moaning, and Bailey carried the cause of the trouble over to the

251

window and threw it out.

But the result of the absurd incident was a further destruction of their morale. Even Beresford, so far calm with the quiet of the virtuous onlooker, was now pallid in the light of the matches they successively lighted. And onto this strained situation came at last Billy and the Unknown.

The Unknown still wore his air of dazed bewilderment, true or feigned, but at least he was not able to walk without support. They stared at him, at his tattered, muddy garments, at the threads of rope still clinging to his ankles—and wondered. He returned their stares vacantly.

"Come in," began Miss Cornelia. "Sit down." He obeyed both commands docilely enough.

"Are you better now?"

"Somewhat." His words still came very slowly.

"Billy, you can go."

"I stay, please!" said Billy wistfully, making no movement to leave. His gesture toward the darkness of the corridor spoke louder than words.

Bailey watched him, suspicion dawning in his eyes. He could not account for the butler's inexplicable terror of being left alone.

"Anderson intimated that the doctor had an accomplice in this house," he said, crossing to Billy and taking him by the arm. "Why isn't this the man?" Billy cringed away. "Please, no," he begged pitifully.

Bailey turned him around so that he faced the

Hidden Room.

"Did you know that room was there?" he questioned, his doubts still unquieted.

Billy shook his head.

"No."

"He couldn't have locked us in," said Miss Cornelia. "He was *with* us."

Bailey demurred, not to her remark itself, but to its implication of Billy's entire innocence.

"He may *know* who did it. Do you?"

Billy shook his head.

Bailey remained unconvinced.

"Who did you see at the head of the small staircase?" he queried imperatively. "Now we're through with nonsense; I want the truth!"

Billy shivered.

"See face—that's all," he brought out at last.

"*Whose* face?"

Again it was evident that Billy knew or thought he knew more than he was willing to tell.

"Don't know," he said with obvious untruth, looking down at the floor.

"Never mind, Billy," cut in Miss Cornelia. To her mind questioning Billy was wasting time. She looked at the Unknown.

"Solve the mystery of *this* man and we may get at the facts," she said in accents of conviction.

As Bailey turned toward her questioningly, Billy attempted to steal silently out of the door, apparently preferring any fears that might lurk in the darkness of the corridor to a further grilling on the subject of whom or what he had seen on the alcove stairs. But Bailey caught the movement out of the tail of his eye.

"You stay here," he commanded. Billy stood frozen.

Beresford raised the candle so that it cast its light full in the Unknown's face.

"This chap claims to have lost his memory," he said dubiously. "I suppose a blow on the head might do that, I don't know."

"I wish somebody would knock *me* on the head! *I'd* like to forget a few things!" moaned Lizzie, but the interruption went unregarded.

"Don't you even know your name?" queried Miss Cornelia of the Unknown.

The Unknown shook his head with a slow, laborious gesture.

"Not—yet."

"Or where you came from?"

Once more the battered head made its movement of negation.

"Do you remember how you got in this house?" The Unknown made an effort.

"Yes—I—remember—that—all—right—" he said, apparently undergoing an enormous strain in order to make himself speak at all. He put his hand to his head.

"My—head—aches—to—beat—the—band," he continued slowly.

Miss Cornelia was at a loss. If this were acting, it was at least fine acting.

"How did you happen to come to this house?" she persisted, her voice unconsciously tuning itself to the slow, laborious speech of the Unknown.

"Saw—the—lights."

Bailey broke in with a question.

"Where were you when you saw the lights?"

The Unknown wet his lips with his tongue, painfully.

"I—broke—out—of—the—garage," he said at length.

This was unexpected. A general movement of interest ran over the group.

"How did you get there?" Beresford took his turn as questioner.

The Unknown shook his head, so slowly and deliberately that Miss Cornelia's fingers itched to shake him in spite of his injuries.

"I—don't—know."

"Have you been robbed?" queried Bailey with keen suspicion.

The Unknown mumbled something unintelligible. Then he seemed to get command of his tongue again.

"Everything gone—out of—my pockets," he said.

"Including your watch?" pursued Bailey, remembering the watch that Beresford had found in the grounds.

The Unknown would neither affirm nor deny.

255

"If — I — had — a — watch — it's gone," he said with maddening deliberation. "All my — papers — are gone."

Miss Cornelia pounced upon this last statement like a cat upon a mouse.

"How do you know you *had* papers?" she asked sharply.

For the first time the faintest flicker of a smile seemed to appear for a moment on the Unknown's features. Then it vanished as abruptly as it had come.

"Most men — carry papers — don't they?" he asked, staring blindly in front of him. "I'm dazed — but — my mind's — all — right. If you — ask me — I — think — I'm — d-damned funny!"

He gave the ghost of a chuckle. Bailey and Beresford exchanged glances.

"Did you ring the house phone?" insisted Miss Cornelia.

The Unknown nodded.

"Yes."

Miss Cornelia and Bailey gave each other a look of wonderment.

"I — leaned against — the button — in the garage —" he went on. "Then — I think — maybe I — fainted. That's not clear."

His eyelids drooped. He seemed about to faint again.

Dale rose, and came over to him, with a sympathetic movement of her hand.

"You don't remember how you were hurt?" she asked gently.

The Unknown stared ahead of him, his eyes filming, as if he were trying to puzzle it out.

"No," he said at last. "The first thing I remember — I was in the garage — tied." He moved his lips. "I was — gagged — too — that's — what's the matter — with my tongue — now — Then — I got myself — free — and — got out — of a window — "

Miss Cornelia made a movement to question him further. Beresford stopped her with his hand uplifted.

"Just a moment, Miss Van Gorder. Anderson ought to know of this."

He started for the door without perceiving the flash of keen intelligence and alertness that had lit the Unknown's countenance for an instant, as once before, at the mention of the detective's name. But just as he reached the door the detective entered.

He halted for a moment, staring at the strange figure of the Unknown.

"A new element in our mystery, Mr. Anderson," said Miss Cornelia, remembering that the detective might not have heard of the mysterious stranger before — as he had been locked in the billiard room when the latter had made his queer entrance.

The detective and the Unknown gazed at each other for a moment — the Unknown with his old expression of vacant stupidity.

"Quite dazed, poor fellow," Miss Cornelia went

257

on.

Beresford added other words of explanation.

"He doesn't remember what happened to him. Curious, isn't it?"

The detective still seemed puzzled.

"How did he get into the house?"

"He came through the terrace door some time ago," answered Miss Cornelia. "Just before we were locked in."

Her answer seemed to solve the problem to Anderson's satisfaction.

"Doesn't remember anything, eh?" he said dryly. He crossed over to the mysterious stranger and put his hand under the Unknown's chin, jerking his head up roughly.

"Look up here!" he commanded.

The Unknown stared at him for an instant with blank, vacuous eyes. Then his head dropped back upon his breast again.

"Look up, you —" muttered the detective, jerking his head again. "This losing your memory stuff doesn't go down with me!" His eyes bored into the Unknown's.

"It doesn't — go down — very well — with me — either," said the Unknown weakly, making no movement of protest against Anderson's rough handling.

"Did you ever see me before?" demanded the latter. Beresford held the candle closer so that he might watch the Unknown's face for any involuntary movement of betrayal.

But the Unknown made no such movement. He gazed at Anderson, apparently with the greatest bewilderment, then his eyes cleared, he seemed to be about to remember who the detective was.

"You're — the — doctor — I — saw — downstairs — aren't you?" he said innocently. The detective set his jaw. He started off on a new tack.

"Does this belong to you?" he said suddenly, plucking from his pocket the battered gold watch that Beresford had found and waving it before the Unknown's blank face.

The Unknown stared at it a moment, as a child might stare at a new toy, with no gleam of recognition. Then —

"Maybe," he admitted. "I — don't — know."

His voice trailed off. He fell back against Bailey's arm.

Miss Cornelia gave a little shiver. The third degree in reality was less pleasant to watch than it had been to read about in the pages of her favorite detective stories.

"He's evidently been attacked," she said, turning to Anderson. "He claims to have recovered consciousness in the garage where he was tied hand and foot!"

"He does, eh?" said the detective heavily. He glared at the Unknown. "If you'll give me five minutes alone with him, I'll get the *truth* out of him!" he promised.

A look of swift alarm swept over the Unknown's face at the words, unperceived by any except Miss Cornelia. The others started obediently to yield to the detective's behest and leave him alone with his prisoner. Miss Cornelia was the first to move toward the door. On her way, she turned.

"Do you believe that money is irrevocably gone?" she asked of Anderson.

The detective smiled.

"There's no such word as 'irrevocable' in my vocabulary," he answered. "But I believe it's out of the house, if that's what you mean."

Miss Cornelia still hesitated, on the verge of departure.

"Suppose I tell you that there are certain facts that you have overlooked?" she said slowly.

"Still on the trail!" muttered the detective sardonically. He did not even glance at her. He seemed only anxious that the other members of the group would get out of his way for once and leave him a clear field for his work.

"I was right about the doctor, wasn't I?" she insisted.

"Just fifty per cent right," said Anderson crushingly. "And the doctor didn't turn that trick alone. Now—" he went on with weary patience, "if you'll *all* go out and close that door—"

Miss Cornelia, defeated, took a candle from Bailey and stepped into the corridor. Her figure stiffened. She gave an audible gasp of dismayed surprise.

"Quick!" she cried, turning back to the others and gesturing toward the corridor. "A man just went through that skylight and out onto the roof!"

Chapter Nineteen: Murder on Murder

"Out on the roof!"

"Come on Beresford!"

"Hustle—you men! He may be armed!"

"Righto—coming!"

And following Miss Cornelia's lead, Jack Bailey, Anderson, Beresford, and Billy dashed out into the corridor, leaving Dale and the frightened Lizzie alone with the Unknown.

"And *I'd* run if my legs would!" Lizzie despaired.

"Hush!" said Dale, her ears strained for sounds of conflict. Lizzie, creeping closer to her for comfort, stumbled over one of the Unknown's feet and promptly set up a new wail.

"How do we know this fellow right here isn't *the Bat?*" she asked in a blood-chilling whisper, nearly stabbing the unfortunate Unknown in the eye with her thumb as she pointed at him. The Unknown was either too dazed or too crafty to make any answer. His silence confirmed Lizzie's worst suspicions. She fairly hugged the floor and began to pray in a whisper.

Miss Cornelia re-entered cautiously with her candle, closing the door gently behind her as she came.

"What did you see?" gasped Dale.

Miss Cornelia smiled broadly.

"I didn't see anything," she admitted with the greatest calm. "I had to get that dratted detective out of the room before I assassinated him."

"Nobody went through the skylight?" said Dale incredulously.

"They have now," answered Miss Cornelia with obvious satisfaction. "The whole outfit of them."

She stole a glance at the veiled eyes of the Unknown. He was lying limply back in his chair, as if the excitement had been too much for him, and yet she could have sworn she had seen him leap to his feet, like a man in full possession of his faculties, when she had given her false cry of alarm.

"Then why did you—" began Dale dazedly, unable to fathom her aunt's reasons for her trick.

"Because," interrupted Miss Cornelia decidedly, "that money's in this room. If the man who took it out of the safe got away with it, why did he come back and hide there?"

Her forefinger jabbed at the hidden chamber wherein the masked intruder had terrified Dale with threats of instant death.

"He got it out of the safe—and that's as far as he *did* get with it," she persisted inexorably. "There's a *hat* behind that safe, a man's felt hat!"

So this was the discovery she had hinted of to Anderson before he rebuffed her proffer of assistance!

"Oh, I wish he'd take his hat and go home!" groaned Lizzie inattentive to all but her own fears.

Miss Cornelia did not even bother to rebuke her. She crossed behind the wicker clothes hamper and picked up something from the floor.

"A half-burned candle," she mused. "Another thing the detective overlooked."

She stepped back to the center of the room, looking knowingly from the candle to the Hidden Room and back again.

"Oh, my God—another one!" shrieked Lizzie as the dark shape of a man appeared suddenly outside the window, as if materialized from the air.

Miss Cornelia snatched up the revolver from the top of the hamper.

"Don't shoot, it's Jack!" came a warning cry from Dale as she recognized the figure of her lover.

Miss Cornelia laid her revolver down on the hamper again. The vacant eyes of the Unknown caught the movement.

Bailey swung in through the window, panting a little from his exertions.

"The man Lizzie saw drop from the skylight undoubtedly got to the roof from this window," he said. "It's quite easy."

"But not with one hand," said Miss Cornelia, with her gaze now directed at the row of tall closets around the walls of the room. "When that detective comes back I may have a surprise party for him," she muttered, with a gleam of hope in her eye.

Dale explained the situation to Jack.

"Aunt Cornelia thinks the money's still here."

Miss Cornelia snorted.

"I *know* it's here." She started to open the closets, one after the other, beginning at the left. Bailey saw what she was doing and began to help her.

Not so Lizzie. She sat on the floor in a heap, her eyes riveted on the Unknown, who in his turn was gazing at Miss Cornelia's revolver on the hamper with the intent stare of a baby or an idiot fascinated by a glittering piece of glass.

Dale noticed the curious tableau.

"Lizzie, what are you looking at?" she said with a nervous shake in her voice.

"What's *he* looking at?" asked Lizzie sepulchrally, pointing at the Unknown. Her pointed forefinger drew his eyes away from the revolver; he sank back into his former apathy, listless, drooping.

Miss Cornelia rattled the knob of a high closet by the other wall.

"This one is locked and the key's gone," she announced. A new flicker of interest grew in the eyes of the Unknown. Lizzie glanced away from him, terrified.

"If there's anything locked up in that closet," she whimpered, "you'd better let it stay! There's enough running loose in this house as it is!"

265

Unfortunately for her, her whimper drew Miss Cornelia's attention upon her.

"Lizzie, did you ever take that key?" the latter queried sternly.

"No'm," said Lizzie, too scared to dissimulate if she had wished. She wagged her head violently a dozen times, like a china figure on a mantelpiece.

Miss Cornelia pondered.

"It may be locked from the inside; I'll soon find out." She took a wire hairpin from her hair and pushed it through the keyhole. But there was no key on the other side; the hairpin went through without obstruction. Repeated efforts to jerk the door open failed. And finally Miss Cornelia bethought herself of a key from the other closet doors.

Dale and Lizzie on one side, Bailey on the other, collected the keys of the other closets from their locks while Miss Cornelia stared at the one whose doors were closed as if she would force its secret from it with her eyes. The Unknown had been so quiet during the last few minutes, that, unconsciously, the others had ceased to pay much attention to him, except the casual attention one devotes to a piece of furniture. Even Lizzie's eyes were now fixed on the locked closet. And the Unknown himself was the first to notice this.

At once his expression altered to one of cunning—cautiously, with infinite patience, he began to inch his chair over toward the wicker clothes hamper. The noise of the others, moving about the room, drowned out what little he made in moving his chair.

At last he was within reach of the revolver. His hand shot out in one swift sinuous thrust, clutched the weapon, withdrew. He then concealed the revolver among his tattered garments as best he could and, cautiously as before, inched his chair back again to its original position. When the others noticed him again, the mask of lifelessness was back on his face and one could have sworn he had not changed his position by the breadth of an inch.

"There, that unlocked it!" cried Miss Cornelia triumphantly at last, as the key to one of the other closet doors slid smoothly into the lock and she heard the click that meant victory.

She was about to throw open the closet door. But Bailey motioned her back.

"I'd keep *back* a little," he cautioned. "You don't know what may be inside."

"Mercy sakes, who wants to know?" shivered Lizzie. Dale and Miss Cornelia, too, stepped aside involuntarily as Bailey took the candle and prepared, with a good deal of caution, to open the closet door.

The door swung open at last. He could look in. He did so—and stared appalled at what he saw, while goose flesh crawled on his spine and the hairs of his head stood up.

After a moment he closed the door of the closet and turned back, white-faced, to the others.

"What is it?" said Dale aghast. "What did you see?"

Bailey found himself unable to answer for a moment. Then he pulled himself together. He turned to Miss Van Gorder.

"Miss Cornelia, I think we have found the ghost the Jap butler saw," he said slowly. "How are your nerves?"

Miss Cornelia extended a hand that did not tremble.

"Give me the candle."

He did so. She went to the closet and opened the door.

Whatever faults Miss Cornelia may have had, lack of courage was not one of them—or the ability to withstand a stunning mental shock. Had it been otherwise she might well have crumpled to the floor, as if struck down by an invisible hammer, the moment the closet door swung open before her.

Huddled on the floor of the closet was the body of a man. So crudely had he been crammed into this hiding-place that he lay twisted and bent. And as if to add to the horror of the moment one arm, released from its confinement, now slipped and slid out into the floor of the room.

Miss Cornelia's voice sounded strange to her own ears when finally she spoke.

"But who is it?"

"It is—or was—Courtleigh Flemming," said Bailey dully.

"But how can it be? Mr. Fleming died two weeks ago. I—"

"He died in this house sometime tonight. The body is still warm."

"But who killed him? The Bat?"

"Isn't it likely that the doctor did it? The man who has been his accomplice all along? Who probably bought a cadaver out West and buried it with honors here not long ago?"

He spoke without bitterness. Whatever resentment he might have felt died in that awful presence.

"He got into the house early tonight," he said, "probably with the doctor's connivance. That wrist watch there is probably the luminous eye Lizzie thought she saw."

But Miss Cornelia's face was still thoughtful, and he went on:

"Isn't it clear, Miss Van Gorder?" he queried, with a smile. "The doctor and old Mr. Fleming formed a conspiracy, both needed money, lots of it. Fleming was to rob the bank and hide the money here. Well's part was to issue a false death certificate in the West, and bury a substitute body, secured God knows how. It was easy; it kept the name of the president of the Union Bank free from suspicion—and it put the blame on me."

He paused, thinking it out.

"Only they slipped up in one place. Dick Fleming leased the house to you and they couldn't get it back."

"Then you are sure," said Miss Cornelia quickly, "that tonight Courtleigh Fleming broke in, with the doctor's assistance—and that he killed Dick, his own nephew, from the staircase?"

"Aren't you?" asked Bailey surprised. The more he thought of it the less clearly could he visualize it any other way.

Miss Cornelia shook her head decidedly.

"No."

Bailey thought her merely obstinate—unwilling to give up, for pride's sake, her own pet theory of the activities of the Bat.

"Wells tried to get out of the house tonight with that blueprint. *Why?* Because he knew the moment we got it, we'd come up here—and Fleming was here."

"Perfectly true," nodded Miss Cornelia. "And then?"

"Old Fleming killed Dick and Wells killed Fleming," said Bailey succinctly. "You can't get away from it!"

But Miss Cornelia still shook her head. The explanation was too mechanical. It laid too little emphasis on the characters of those most concerned.

"No," she said. "No. The doctor isn't a murderer. He's as puzzled as we are about some things. He and Courtleigh Fleming were working together but remember this—Doctor Wells was locked in the living-room with us. He'd been trying to get up the stairs all evening and failed every time."

270

But Bailey was as convinced of the truth of his theory as she of hers.

"He was here ten minutes ago, locked in this room," he said with a glance at the ladder up which the doctor had ascended.

"I'll grant you that," said Miss Cornelia. "But—" She thought back swiftly. "But at the same time an Unknown Masked Man was locked in that mantel-room with Dale. The doctor put out the candle when you opened that Hidden Room. *Why? Because he thought Courtleigh Fleming was hiding there?*" Now the missing pieces of her puzzle were falling into their places with a vengeance. "But at this moment," she continued, "the doctor believes that Fleming has made his escape! No, we haven't solved the mystery yet. There's another element—an *unknown* element," her eyes rested for a moment upon the Unknown, "and that element is—the Bat!"

She paused, impressively. The others stared at her, no longer able to deny the sinister plausibility of her theory. But this new tangling of the mystery, just when the black threads seemed raveled out at last, was almost too much for Dale.

"Oh, call the detective!" she stammered, on the verge of hysterical tears. "Let's get through with this thing! I can't bear any more!"

But Miss Cornelia did not even hear her. Her mind, strung now to concert pitch, had harked back to the point it had reached some time ago, and which all recent distractions had momentarily oblit-

271

erated.

Had the money been taken out of the house or had it not? In that mad rush for escape had the man hidden with Dale in the recess back of the mantel carried his booty with him, or left it behind? It was not in the Hidden Room, that was certain.

Yet she was so hopeless by that time that her first search was purely perfunctory.

During her progress about the room the Unknown's eyes followed her, but so still had he sat, so amazing had been the discovery of the body, that no one any longer observed him. Now and then his head drooped forward as if actual weakness was almost overpowering him, but his eyes were keen and observant, and he was no longer taking the trouble to act—if he had been acting.

It was when Bailey finally opened the lid of a clothes hamper that they stumbled on their first clue.

"Nothing here but some clothes and books," he said, glancing inside.

"Books?" said Miss Cornelia dubiously. "I left no books in that hamper."

Bailey picked up one of the cheap paper novels and read its title aloud, with a wry smile.

"Little Rosebud's Lover, Or The Cruel Revenge," by Laura Jean—"

"That's mine!" said Lizzie promptly. "Oh, Miss Neily, I tell you this house *is* haunted. I left that

272

book in my satchel along with *Wedded But No Wife* and now—"

"Where's your satchel?" snapped Miss Cornelia, her eyes gleaming.

"Where's my satchel?" mumbled Lizzie, staring about as best she could. "I don't see it. If that wretch has stolen my satchel—!"

"Where did you leave it?"

"Up here. Right in this room. It was a new satchel too. I'll have the law on him, that's what I'll do."

"Isn't that your satchel, Lizzie?" asked Miss Cornelia, indicating a battered bag in a dark corner of shadows above the window.

Lizzie approached it gingerly.

"Yes'm," she admitted. But she did not dare approach very close to the recovered bag. It might bite her!

"Put it there on the hamper," ordered Miss Cornelia.

"I'm scared to touch it!" moaned Lizzie. "It may have a bomb in it!"

She took up the bag between finger and thumb and, holding it with the care she would have bestowed upon a bottle of nitroglycerin, carried it over to the hamper and set it down. Then she backed away from it, ready to leap for the door at a moment's warning.

Miss Cornelia started for the satchel. Then she remembered. She turned to Bailey.

273

"You open it," she said graciously. "If the money's there you're the one who ought to find it."

Bailey gave her a look of gratitude. Then, smiling at Dale encouragingly, he crossed over to the satchel, Dale at his heels. Miss Cornelia watched him fumble at the catch of the bag—even Lizzie drew closer. For a moment even the Unknown was forgotten.

Bailey gave a triumphant cry.

"The money's here!"

"Oh, thank God!" sobbed Dale.

It was an emotional moment. It seemed to have penetrated even through the haze enveloping the injured man in his chair. Slowly he got up, like a man who has been waiting for his moment, and now that it had come was in no hurry about it. With equal deliberation he drew the revolver and took a step forward. And at that instant a red glare appeared outside the open window and overhead could be heard the feet of the searchers, running.

"Fire!" screamed Lizzie, pointing to the window, even as Beresford's voice from the roof rang out in a shout. "The garage is burning!"

They turned toward the door to escape, but a strange and menacing figure blocked their way.

It was the Unknown, no longer the bewildered stranger who had stumbled in through the living-room door but a man with every faculty of mind and body alert and the light of a deadly purpose in his eyes. He covered the group with Miss Cornelia's

274

revolver.

"This door is locked and the key is in my pocket!" he said in a savage voice as the red light at the window grew yet more vivid and muffled cries and tramplings from overhead betokened universal confusion and alarm.

Chapter Twenty: "He Is—The Bat!"

Lizzie opened her mouth to scream. But for once she did not carry out her purpose.

"Not a sound out of *you!*" warned the Unknown brutally, almost jabbing the revolver into her ribs. He wheeled on Bailey.

"Close that satchel," he commanded, "and put it back where you found it!"

Bailey's fist closed. He took a step toward his captor.

"*You—*" he began in a furious voice. But the steely glint in the eyes of the Unknown was enough to give any man pause.

"Jack!" pleaded Dale. Bailey halted.

"Do what he tells you!" Miss Cornelia insisted, her voice shaking.

A brave man may be willing to fight with odds a hundred to one but only a fool will rush on certain death. Reluctantly, dejectedly, Bailey obeyed— stuffed the money back in the satchel and replaced the latter in its corner of shadows near the window.

"It's the Bat—it's the Bat!" whispered Lizzie eerily, and, for once her gloomy prophecies seemed to be in a fair way of justification, for "Blow out that candle!" commanded the Unknown sternly, and, after a moment of hesitation as Miss Cornelia's part, the room was again plunged in darkness except for the red glow at the window.

This finished Lizzie for the evening. She spoke from a dry throat.

"I'm going to scream!" she sobbed hysterically. "I can't keep it back!"

But at last she had encountered someone who had no patience with her vagaries.

"Put that woman in the mantel-room and shut her up!" ordered the Unknown, the muzzle of his revolver emphasizing his words with a savage little movement.

Bailey took Lizzie under the arms and started to execute the order. But the sometime colleen from Kerry did not depart without one Parthian arrow.

"Don't shove," she said in tones of the greatest dignity as she stumbled into the Hidden Room. "I'm damn glad to go!"

The iron doors shut behind her. Bailey watched the Unknown intently. One moment of relaxed vigilance and—

But though the Unknown was unlocking the door with his left hand the revolver in his right hand was as steady as a rock. He seemed to listen for a moment at the crack of the door.

"Not a sound if you value your lives!" he warned again. He shepherded them away from the direction of the window with his revolver.

"In a moment or two," he said in a hushed, taut voice, "a man will come into this room, either through the door or by that window—the man who started the fire to draw you out of this house."

Bailey threw aside all pride in his concern for Dale's safety.

"For God's sake, don't keep these women here!" he pleaded in low, tense tones.

The Unknown seemed to tower above him like a destroying angel.

"Keep them here where we can watch them!" he whispered with fierce impatience. "Don't you understand? There's a *killer* loose!"

And so for a moment they stood there, waiting for they knew not what. So swift had been the transition from joy to deadly terror, and now to suspense, that only Miss Cornelia's agile brain seemed able to respond.

"I begin to understand," she said in a low tone. "The man who struck you down and tied you in the garage—the man who killed Dick Fleming and stabbed that poor wretch in the closet—the man who locked us in downstairs and removed the money from that safe—the man who started the fire outside—is—"

"Sssh!" warned the Unknown imperatively as a

278

sound from the direction of the window seemed to reach his ears. He ran quickly back to the corridor door and locked it.

"Stand back out of that light! The ladder!"

Miss Cornelia and Dale shrank back against the mantel. Bailey took up a post beside the window, the Unknown flattening himself against the wall beside him. There was a breathless pause.

The top of the extension ladder began to tremble. A black bulk stood clearly outlined against the diminishing red glow—the Bat, masked and sinister, on his last foray!

There was no sound as the killer stepped into the room. He waited for a second that seemed a year—still no sound. Then he turned cautiously toward the place where he had left the satchel—the beam of his flashlight picked it out.

In an instant the Unknown and Bailey were upon him. There was a short, ferocious struggle in the darkness, a gasp of laboring lungs, the thud of fighting bodies clenched in a death grapple.

"Get his gun!" muttered the Unknown hoarsely to Bailey as he tore the Bat's lean hands away from his throat. "Got it?"

"Yes," gasped Bailey. He jabbed the muzzle against a straining back. The Bat ceased to struggle. Bailey stepped a little away.

"I've still got you covered!" he said fiercely. The Bat made no sound.

"Hold out your hands, Bat, while I put on the

279

bracelets," commanded the Unknown in tones of terse triumph. He snapped the steel cuffs on the wrists of the murderous prowler. "Sometimes even the cleverest Bat comes through a window at night and is caught. Double murder—burglary—and arson! That's a good night's work even for you, Bat!"

He switched his flashlight on the Bat's masked face. As he did so the house lights came on; the electric light company had at last remembered its duties. All blinked for an instant in the sudden illumination.

"Take off that handkerchief!" barked the Unknown, motioning at the black silk handkerchief that still hid the face of the Bat from recognition. Bailey stripped it from the haggard, desperate features with a quick movement—and stood appalled.

A simultaneous gasp went up from Dale and Miss Cornelia.

It was Anderson, the detective! And he was—the Bat!

"It's Mr. Anderson!" stuttered Dale, aghast at the discovery.

The Unknown gloated over his captive.

"*I'm* Anderson," he said. "This man has been impersonating me. You're a good actor, Bat, for a fellow that's such a *bad* actor!" he taunted. "How did you get the dope on this case? Did you tap the wires to headquarters?"

The Bat allowed himself a little sardonic smile.

"I'll tell you that when I—" he began, then, suddenly, made his last bid for freedom. With one swift, desperate movement, in spite of his handcuffs, he jerked the real Anderson's revolver from him by the barrel, then wheeling with lightning rapidity on Bailey, brought the butt of Anderson's revolver down on his wrist. Bailey's revolver fell to the floor with a clatter. The Bat swung toward the door. Again the tables were turned!

"Hands up, everybody!" he ordered, menacing the group with the stolen pistol. "Hands up—you!" as Miss Cornelia kept her hands at her sides.

It was the greatest moment of Miss Cornelia's life.

She smiled sweetly and came toward the Bat as if the pistol aimed at her heart were as innocuous as a toothbrush.

"Why?" she queried mildly. "I took the bullets out of that revolver two hours ago."

The Bat flung the revolver toward her with a curse. The real Anderson instantly snatched up the gun that Bailey had dropped and covered the Bat.

"Don't move!" he warned, "or I'll fill you full of lead!" He smiled out of the corner of his mouth at Miss Cornelia who was primly picking up the revolver that the Bat had flung at her—her own revolver.

"You see—you never know what a woman will do," he continued.

Miss Cornelia smiled. She broken open the revolver, five loaded shells fell from it to the floor.

The Bat stared at her, then stared incredulously at the bullets.

"You see," she said, "I, too, have a little imagination!"

Chapter Twenty-one: Quite A Collection

An hour or so later, in a living-room whose terrors had departed, Miss Cornelia, her niece, and Jack Bailey were gathered before a roaring fire. The local police had come and gone; the bodies of Courtleigh Fleming and his nephew had been removed to the mortuary; Beresford had returned to his home, though under summons as a material witness; the Bat, under heavy guard, had gone off under charge of the detective. As for Doctor Wells, he too was under arrest, and a broken man, though, considering the fact that Courtleigh Fleming had been throughout the prime mover in the conspiracy, he might escape with a comparatively light sentence. In a little while the newspapermen of all the great journals would be at the door — but for a moment the sorely tried group at Cedarcrest enjoyed a temporary respite and they made the best of it while they could.

The fire burned brightly and the lovers, hand in hand, sat before it. But Miss Cornelia, birdlike and brisk, sat upright on a chair near by and relived the greatest triumph of her life while she knitted with automatic precision.

"Knit two, purl two," she would say, and then would wander once more back to the subject in hand. Out behind the flower garden the ruins of the garage and her beloved car were still smoldering; a cool night wind came through the broken window-pane where not so long before the bloody hand of the injured detective had intruded itself. On the door to the hall, still fastened as the Bat had left it, was the pathetic little creature with which the Bat had signed a job—for once, before he had completed it.

But calmly and dispassionately Miss Cornelia worked out the crossword puzzle of the evening and announced her results.

"It is all clear," she said. "Of course the doctor had the blueprint. And the Bat tried to get it from him. Then when the doctor had stunned him and locked him in the billiard room, the Bat still had the key and unlocked his own handcuffs. After that he had only to get out of a window and shut us in here."

And again:

"He had probably trailed the real detective all the way from town and attacked him where Mr. Beresford found the watch."

Once, too, she harkened back to the anonymous letters.

"It must have been a blow to the doctor and Courtleigh Fleming when they found me settled in the house!" She smiled grimly. "And when their letters failed to dislodge me."

But it was the Bat who held her interest; his daring assumption of the detective's identity, his searching of the house ostensibly for their safety but in reality for the treasure, and that one moment of irresolution when he did not shoot the doctor at the top of the ladder. And thereafter lost his chance.

It somehow weakened her terrified admiration for him, but she had nothing but acclaim for the escape he had made from the Hidden Room itself.

"That took brains," she said. "Cold, hard brains. To dash out of that room and down the stairs, pull off his mask and pick up a candle, and then to come calmly back to the trunk room again and accuse the doctor. That took real ability. But I dread to think what would have happened when he asked us all to go out and leave him alone with the real Anderson!"

It was after two o'clock when she finally sent the young people off to get some needed sleep but she herself was still bright-eyed and wide-awake.

When Lizzie came at last to coax and scold her into bed, she was sitting happily at the table surrounded by divers small articles which she was handling with an almost childlike zest. A clipping about the Bat from the evening newspaper; a piece of paper on which was a well-defined fingerprint; a revolver and a heap of five shells; a small very dead bat; the anonymous warnings, including the stone in which the last one had been wrapped; a battered and broken watch, somehow left behind; a dried and broken dinner roll; and the box of sedative powders brought by Doctor Wells.

Lizzie came over to the table and surveyed her grimly.

"You see, Lizzie, it's quite a collection. I'm going to take them and—"

But Lizzie bent over the table and picked up the box of powders.

"No, ma'am," she said with extreme finality. "You are not. You are going to take these and go to bed."

And Miss Cornelia did.

DORIS MILES DISNEY IS
THE QUEEN OF SUSPENSE

DO NOT FOLD, SPINDLE OR MUTILATE (2154, $2.95)
Even at 58, Sophie Tate Curtis was always clowning—sending her
bridge club into stitches by filling out a computer dating service
card with a phony name. But her clowning days were about to
come to an abrupt end. For one of her computer-suitors was very,
very serious—and he would make sure that this was Sophie's last
laugh . . .

MRS. MEEKER'S MONEY (2212, $2.95)
It took old Mrs. Meeker $30,000 to realize that she was being swin-
dled by a private detective. Bent on justice, she turned to Postal
Inspector Madden. But—unfortunately for Mrs. Meeker—this
case was about to provide Madden with a change of pace by turning from mail fraud into murder, C.O.D.

HERE LIES (2362, $2.95)
Someone was already occupying the final resting place of the late
Mrs. Phoebe Upton Clarke. A stranger had taken up underground
residence there more than 45 years earlier—an illegal squatter with
no name—and a bullet in his skull!

THE LAST STRAW (2286, $2.95)
Alone with a safe containing over $30,000 worth of bonds, Dean
Lipscomb couldn't help remembering that he needed a little extra
money. The bonds were easily exchanged for cash, but Leonard
Riggott discovered them missing sooner than Dean expected. One
crime quickly led to another . . . but this time Dean discovered
that it was easier to redeem the bonds than himself!

*Available wherever paperbacks are sold, or order direct from the
Publisher. Send cover price plus 50¢ per copy for mailing and handling to Zebra Books, Dept. 2627, 475 Park Avenue South, New
York, N.Y. 10016. Residents of New York, New Jersey and Pennsylvania must include sales tax. DO NOT SEND CASH.*

MYSTERIES TO KEEP YOU GUESSING
by John Dickson Carr

CASTLE SKULL (1974, $3.50)

The hand may be quicker than the eye, but ghost stories didn't hoodwink Henri Bencolin. A very real murderer was afoot in Castle Skull—a murderer who must be found before he strikes again.

IT WALKS BY NIGHT (1931, $3.50)

The police burst in and found the Duc's severed head staring at them from the center of the room. Both the doors had been guarded, yet the murderer had gone in and out *without having been seen*!

THE EIGHT OF SWORDS (1881, $3.50)

The evidence showed that while waiting to kill Mr. Depping, the murderer had calmly eaten his victim's dinner. But before famed crime-solver Dr. Gideon Fell could serve up the killer to Scotland Yard, there would be another course of murder.

THE MAN WHO COULD NOT SHUDDER (1703, $3.50)

Three guests at Martin Clarke's weekend party swore they saw the pistol lifted from the wall, levelled, and shot. *Yet no hand held it*. It couldn't have happened—but there was a dead body on the floor to prove that it had.

THE PROBLEM OF THE WIRE CAGE (1702, $3.50)

There was only one set of footsteps in the soft clay surface— and those footsteps belonged to the victim. It seemed impossible to prove that anyone had killed Frank Dorrance.

Available wherever paperbacks are sold, or order direct from the Publisher. Send cover price plus 50¢ per copy for mailing and handling to Zebra Books, Dept. 2627, 475 Park Avenue South, New York, N.Y. 10016. Residents of New York, New Jersey and Pennsylvania must include sales tax. DO NOT SEND CASH.